THE COLOR SEXY

Edited By
MARCUS ANTHONY

Herndon, VA

Published in the United States by STARbooks Press

PO Box 711612, Herndon, VA 20171

Many thanks to graphic artist Emma Aldous:
www.arthousepublishing.co.uk

Printed in the United States

Herndon, VA

Titles by Marcus Anthony

The Sweeter the Juice

Tall, Dark & Delicious

Spice Men

Black Dungeon Masters

The Color Sexy

CONTENTS

UNDERCOVER
By Garland

Garland currently lives in Hollywood and is also a fulltime actor. He has written three novels and has short stories in over forty anthologies. www.garlandserotictales.webs.com

I was lying in the bed in complete and utter bliss contentedly puffing my cigarette. I had been in the business longer than I could remember and had never experienced sex like that before. I had fucked hundreds, thousands, of men and had never been with someone like him; he was wild and passionate. Taking another long puff, I rolled the smoke around in my mouth with my tongue before exhaling and looked toward the bathroom. I wondered if he was like that when he was with his wife.

As he turned off the shower, I stubbed out my smoke and stared at the open bathroom door. He stepped into view a few seconds later. A fluffy white towel was wrapped around his waist, contrasting beautifully against his rich mocha colored skin.

My breath caught in my throat, and I felt my cock begin to stir under the motel's thin cheap sheet. He was, without a doubt, the most beautiful man I had ever been with. Perfection is the only word to describe him and even that didn't fully do him justice. Standing tall and proud with an evenly muscled body, he looked like a Greek God.

Letting out a breath, I shook my head. What was going on? I had never felt this way about a client, or any man for that matter. Men bored me. They were only good for one thing; to give me pleasure and keep me in the lifestyle I had grown accustomed to. I had always gone from man to man, discarding them like used underwear. I forgot most of them before they came.

So why was I praying that our time together would never end?

Turning his back to me, he whipped off his towel. I gasped. Good God! His ass was gorgeous. It should be illegal to cover that body with clothes. His cheeks were round and smooth, and his thighs were hard as steel.

Facing me he winked, making me blush.

Throwing the towel on the ground he stood in the doorway and smiled. My heart was beating so fast I was positive I would have a heart attack. His cock was dangling proudly between his legs, a richer mocha color; the same shade as his nipples. He didn't have an inch of body hair, and that turned me on more than he could have known. I loved smooth men.

"Hi cutie," he whispered blowing me a kiss.

I chuckled. "I've been called a lot of names by men over the years, but that's a first."

Never taking his deep, dark eyes off my body, he casually walked toward me. I gulped, nervous and excited as I imagined all the things that could happen.

"I've never done anything like this," he confessed.

"What?" I asked with a flirtatious smile. "Fuck a whore in a cheap motel room? Or fuck a whore that you're supposed to arrest in a cheap motel room?"

"Both," he confessed with a slight chuckle.

"Well I guess this night is full of firsts for both of us," I answered crawling to him and kissing his flat chocolate stomach. There were still little beads of water from his shower. His skin was the smoothest and silkiest I had ever tasted. "Because I've never been with a black man before. And I've never fucked a cop either." I kissed his full juicy lips. "Well not one who was on duty and going to arrest me."

Wrapping his arms around me, we kissed again. His large fingers pinched my back. Our tongues flicked against each other as he gently pushed me back and got on top of me.

"I can't believe this is happening," he whispered, breath sending shivers down my spine. "I've never had any desire to do this. I'm not gay. I'm married."

"Don't worry," I assured him wrapping my arms around him and drawing him down for another kiss. "I won't tell your wife. Breaking up marriages isn't my style."

"I've never cheated on her," he confessed in between kisses.

He ground his hips against me, hard cock pulsing lightly against my navel as his mouth moved down to my neck.

"Mmmmmm … You can't say that anymore," I sighed, squeezing his ass.

As he sucked on my Adam's apple, I closed my eyes in bliss still not believing we had just met a few hours ago. It felt like a lifetime ago. It felt like we were the only people in the world ….

Earlier That Night

It was an unusually slow night. Ever since the invention of Grindr and Adam4Adam, the hustler business was going downhill fast. Men no longer needed to prowl the streets for sex, and thanks to the lousy economy, they were no longer as keen to pay for it as they once were.

Sighing, I checked my phone. It was almost midnight, and I'd only had one client since my shift started. I sighed again. I was twenty-five, practically an old man in hustler years. Maybe I should retire.

I shook my head and chuckled. Retire. That was a laugh. I had no education and the only smarts I did have were street smarts. Sex was all I knew, all I was good at. There was nothing else for me.

3

I could always become a cam model, I thought. Better hours. And wasn't everyone's dream to be able to work at home?

The quick beep beeps of the car horn drew me out of my thoughts. A plain looking beige colored station wagon was parked a few yards away from me. A very hot black guy stared out the driver's side window, eyes glued on me. He looked like an athlete or a model. I smiled. Maybe he had a lot of money. I could jack up my prices.

Giving a little whistle, he signaled me over to the car. Smiling, I walked over to him.

"Evening," I said in my most sultry voice.

"Nice body," he said looking me over with approval.

"Thanks. You should see me without clothes on," I answered making my voice go even huskier.

"Get in." I did. "So how much?"

"Hand job is fifty. Blow job seventy-five. You want me to swallow? The price just went up to a hundred. I'm the best bottom in the business. Clean. Discreet. Completely free of disease, and I plan on staying that way. I don't bareback, no matter how much you offer me. If you want to fuck me, it's two hundred an hour. No exceptions."

The guy smiled. "That's all I needed to know."

Quick as a rattler, he slapped a pair of cold, heavy, metal handcuffs on my wrists.

"What the fuck?" I ejaculated in angered surprise.

Not saying a word, he whipped out of his badge and laughed. I couldn't believe I had been so stupid. I should have smelled him. In all my years, I had never been arrested. Guess my luck had run out, and that made me mad as hell.

"Shit! Fuckin' undercover pig!" I yelled kicking the glove compartment in frustration. The cop laughed harder.

My heart was pounding, and I was sweating from places I didn't even know could sweat.

Okay boy, I silently soothed myself. *Just calm down. You can get out of this.*

I gulped. I prayed I was right.

"Come on man," I finally spoke, grateful my voice didn't waiver. "You don't have to do this. I'm sure we can come to an agreement. I can make you feel good. You'll like it. I promise."

He smirked. "Sorry. Not interested."

"No charge," I blurted out, desperate.

"No chance," he said not missing a beat, keeping his eyes focused on the road ahead.

I sighed. We were silent for what felt like a lifetime. I stared out the window watching the city pass us by. I was running out of time. I had to think of something. Fast.

"Come on," I spoke up again. "Haven't you ever wanted to dominate a white boy? Shove your big black dick up his ass and make him your bitch?"

He grinned as if he were amused; or perhaps pondering my proposition.

I held my breath, waiting to see if he'd bite. He shifted in his seat. Was he aroused? Please God let him be aroused.

"Come on," I continued to prod. "It'll be fun. And nobody has to know. It's win-win."

He nodded his head. Biting my bottom lip, I felt my stomach knot in nervous anticipation.

Turning a corner, he sped up. I held my breath. He didn't stop until he pulled into the parking lot of a cheap motel. I knew the place well.

Oh my God! My eyes bugged out of my head. *Had it really worked?*

Without saying a word, the cop got out of the car and walked into the motel leaving me alone. I didn't like it. The night was quiet. Too quiet. I couldn't even hear any crickets. It was like a scene out of a horror movie.

A few second later, the cop returned and opened my door. He stood there, looking down at me.

"Get out," he commanded softly.

I obeyed.

We didn't say a word as we walked to our room.

When we got into the room, he flicked on the light and took the handcuffs off me.

"Thank you," I said genuinely grateful.

His eyes flashed with lust. Pulling my head to his, he kissed me hard. My body immediately responded with passionate hunger. The cop's arms encircled my body drawing me tight against him. His cock was hard, begging to be free of the confines of his pants. Our kissing grew. His tongue pried open my lips and flicked against mine as he backed me up toward the bed.

Throwing me onto the bed, he stared down at me with want. My chest was rising and falling heavily. I was breathing so hard you'd have thought I had just won The New York City Marathon.

With lighting speed, he undid his belt and tore off his pants. His cock was rock hard. I licked my lips. I couldn't wait to taste that monster.

The cop roughly gripped the back of my head and pulled me toward his dick. Grasping his thick length in his free hand, he ran his silky smooth dick over my eager lips.

"Kiss my dick," he growled voice thick with lust.

Kissing up his length, I wrapped my lips around his mushroom head and slowly lowered my mouth down his shaft. Keeping his hand on my head, he fucked my mouth like a champ. The tip of his dick tickled my tonsils, and his salty-sweet pre-cum seeped into my taste buds as his heavy balls slapped against my chin.

Pulling his cock out of my mouth, he slapped it against my face. I smiled, enjoying feel of it against my flesh.

"Oh you are a little cock whore aren't you?" He chuckled. "Take your clothes off."

My hands were shaking with excitement as I stripped. I couldn't wait to feel that huge tool inside of me.

After he had removed his shirt, he went to the nightstand and took out a bottle of lube and a condom (apparently, he knew this cheap motel's reputation as much as I did). He lathered up his condom-sheathed dick until it glistened.

"Turn over," he said walking back to me, hard cock standing proudly at attention like a soldier ready to march into battle.

I had barely gotten onto my hands and knees before he drizzled the cool lube on my eager hole making it pucker.

My hands gripped the sheets as he pushed into me, stretching out my ass to full capacity. His large hands held onto my hips tightly as he slowly moved his hips back and forth, finding his rhythm. His fingers dug into my flesh as he picked up speed.

7

Closing my eyes, I moaned in pleasure. My dick was hard as stone. The cop was very good in bed, easily the best I'd ever had. He awakened every one of my g-spots and even found some I didn't know I had.

Wrapping my shaggy hair in his fist, he yanked my head back and kissed my neck. I cried out and squeezed my greedy hole around his dick. The cop laughed and nibbled my earlobe.

"You like that?" He asked giving my hair a couple tugs.

"Yeah," I moaned. "Pull my fucking hair."

He slapped my ass making me let out a little pleasurable shriek.

"Don't fucking tell me what to do you little bitch," he growled slapping my ass again. "I'm the top. You're the bottom bitch."

He ground his hips against my ass. The headboard hit the wall, and the mattress squeaked out the rhythm of our fucking. I'm amazed we didn't break the bed.

I moved my ass back and forth, screaming as I shot an impressive load all over the bed. A few seconds later, he pulled out of me, tore the condom off his cock and came on my back, showering me in his cum.

"That was great," he could barely gasp out.

"Yeah," I agreed.

Kissing him, I walked into the bathroom and took a nice long, hot shower.

# # # # #

That memory fueled my passion and desire. Wrapping my arms around him, I dug my nails into his muscular back and kissed his broad shoulders.

"So what happens now?" I sighed, eyes rolling back in my head as he sucked on my neck.

"What do you mean?" He asked looking into my eyes.

"Are you going to arrest me? Lock me up?" I asked not taking my eyes from his.

The cop smiled and tenderly caressed my cheek. "I know I should, but I'm not."

My eyes widened with surprise. I must be a better bottom than I thought!

"Thank you," I said honestly before giving his lips a soft peck.

"Is that your regular corner?" He asked casually.

"Yes. Why?" I asked brow furrowing with confusion.

"I'll see you tomorrow," he responded with a smile, eyes burning with lust. "Same time. Same place."

I smiled, filled with an excitement I had never known.

"Sounds good," I answered.

I had no clue what this was or what was happening but I liked it …

THE OTHER WORLD
By Aiden Lovely

Aiden Lovely resides in New Hampshire. Lovely is a freelance writer who has written many stories. Lovely's work has appeared in many anthologies.

Not a single thought ran through Marcel's mind when his gaze was locked on the dark skin stranger, standing before him. He stood close to the thicket as the sticky air clung to his skin. He lived in the nearby yellow duplex that was now barely visible because of the many trees blocking the view. The woman who lived on the first floor had complained to him about this suspicious stranger standing outside, so he had raced to investigate. The weapon he took with him was now somewhere lost in the grass.

Marcel recognized the man's face from the recurring wet dream he had for the past week, so it was natural for him to be dumbstruck by their unexpected encounter. The stranger didn't exchange any words at first, just a half smile, and then he clutched the sex-starved Marcel's hand, pulling him closer.

"I've been calling you," the stranger said.

Marcel said nothing. Not even in his wildest dreams could he imagine this situation. After the breeze brushed past his skin, a look of surprise and fear washed over his face. What was going on? His heart raced in his chest, giving him a nonthreatening appearance. Honestly, what he lacked in muscle, he made up for in maturity.

"I … see you in my dreams … every night … who … are you?" The words weaseled out of Marcel. Was it possible to have wet dreams about a man he never met? It was difficult to believe, but he couldn't doubt his eyes.

The stranger then said, "Come with me."

Marcel attempted to withdraw his hand, "Hey. Where are you taking me? Let me go."

He didn't want to succumb to temptation, but it was already too late. The man led him further without exchanging anymore words. As the trees buried them, the stranger looked back at Marcel with a lascivious smirk on his face. Suddenly, a bad feeling swirled in Marcel's chest as he disappeared into the darkness of the forest.

The stranger wore a loincloth that hung above his knees. His feet were trapped in gladiator sandals. His body was bulky and dark with skin so smooth like chocolate. His back was decorated in scars and a tattoo circled his upper arm. It was a drawing of an M like character enclosed in a circle. The stranger stopped walking and released Marcel's hand. The man then turned to Marcel with the wilderness in his brass colored eyes.

"I've been calling you in your dreams for the last few nights, waiting for the day I could taste your body in person."

"H-hey," Marcel said. He stepped back. He couldn't even remember the last time a man said something like that to him. He pushed his glasses on his nose. The stranger snatched the glasses off.

"Your glasses cover up your beauty."

"W-who are you?" Marcel said. His bashful heart pounded in his chest. Although Marcel was good looking, he was just an average thin man that spent his days working at the local computer shop. Most guys called him geeky or nerdy, so it was rare for an aggressive stud to bless him with compliments.

The stranger's arms embraced him from the back. He felt the man's hard cock pushing through the fabric. The stranger nibbled on Marcel's ear. Marcel violently flinched.

"What the hell are you doing?" Marcel tried to push the man away, but he lost all strength in his rational thoughts. The man then rested his head on Marcel's shoulder. His hot breath tickled Marcel's earlobe as he said:

"Call me Abassi."

He then shoved Marcel into the thick bush.

The bush wasn't an ordinary plant. It whisked them into a foreign land that Marcel never knew existed.

He stood in the bluish green grass of this unknown world. He used the palm of his hand to block the bright sun from his squinted eyes. What the hell? Where am I? How is this possible? So many questions raced through his mind, but the name, Abassi, spilled from between his lips. His eyes caught Abassi's smoldering gaze. A stare so hot, he imagined it'd burn his clothes off.

Abassi ushered him over to a giant slab of stone. Marcel sat down with his knees pressed tightly together.

"Where on earth am I? Am I even still on earth?"

Abassi laughed at him.

"Welcome to my world," he said, "This is the village of Mataeux."

Abassi opened his arms and spread them far apart as if he were welcoming Marcel. Marcel looked around frantically. The vicious vines hung like snakes through the long branches. The place was made up of jungle from as far as Marcel's eyes could see.

"I've been watching you for a long time," Abassi said, "I want you."

Abassi's fingers crawled up Marcel's arm. Marcel pulled away.

"Why did you bring me here?" he asked.

"You should be honored to be here," Abassi said and then licked his lips at Marcel, "Those dreams you had of us exploring our sexual fantasies – they were real."

Marcel backed up from Abassi, "H-how can that be true? It was just a dream. Dreams aren't real."

"The Mataeux are gifted with the ability to communicate through dreams."

For a moment, Marcel wasn't sure if this were a dream. He looked at Abassi in disbelief.

"Now let me taste you again," Abassi said and snaked his arms around Marcel.

"W-what?"

"Don't say another word," Abassi whispered as he gently massaged Marcel's shoulders. Marcel fell silent as his heart raced in his chest. Abassi pressed his lips lightly against Marcel's. He planted tiny kisses on the man. They were sweet, gentle kisses. Marcel then parted his soft lips, allowing Abassi's tongue to enter. A smothered moan pulled from Marcel's throat. It felt so good to be embraced by Abassi's strong arms. Abassi's warm breaths tickled Marcel's skin as Abassi's natural scent washed over him. Suddenly, Marcel felt overwhelmed with emotion as Abassi's wild tongue slammed against his tongue and filled his mouth. He had a few lovers in the past but none of them made him feel this good.

Abassi massaged Marcel's penis with his hands, roughly rubbing his fingers along the shaft. Marcel trembled. Abassi coated his fingers in a warm lubricant and gently slid one finger in Marcel's body. Marcel jerked and released a heavy gasp. Abassi slid his finger out and then slipped two fingers inside. As he pushed his fingers in deeply, Marcel felt his body surrender to the flooding pleasure.

Abassi then mounted him. His hands slid up Marcel's back and gripped the man's shoulders. He pressed his thick cock against

Marcel's ass. He slid it back and forth between the cheeks. Marcel wanted it badly. As if Abassi read his mind, he massaged Marcel's skin. He then pressed his cock against the tight hole again. The anus shuddered as the tip greeted it.

"Relax."

Abassi's calm voice rested on Marcel's ears. Marcel tried not to tense up so much, but his libido was hostile. Abassi then slipped his throbbing cock inside the inviting entrance. The anus stretched to endure his intruding member. Marcel tensed up. He cringed from the pain as each inch crawled inside him. A ragged moan poured out of his mouth as his body soaked up the pleasure. Warmth spread throughout Marcel. The sloppy noise from the friction and the noise of Abassi's balls slapping against Marcel's flesh echoed throughout the forest. He was embarrassed by the sounds of his moans. He attempted to muffle his voice, but with Abassi pounding him, he could barely control himself.

"You have a lovely voice," Abassi said, "don't hold it back."

Marcel blushed at Abassi's words. He then struggled to control his shuddering body. He felt Abassi's breath on his flesh. Abassi's pace quickened. He pushed his slick cock in deeper. Abassi soothed the body beneath him as he leaned over and dragged his tongue down the man's smooth back.

Marcel couldn't hold back any longer. Abassi pummeled him and gripped his shoulders once again. Marcel pressed his face against the cool slab of stone.

"I'm gonna come," he managed to say. Marcel didn't need to look at Abassi's face to know he was grinning. Abassi pushed in deeper and released a groan as he filled Marcel with his natural juices. Simultaneously, Marcel's cum sprayed out. The milky fluid trailed down the side of the rock.

Abassi slumped over on Marcel. Neither of them said anything. As the two men lay pressed against each other's bare bodies, only the trees towering over them had witnessed their passion. Maybe it was then – right at that moment when Marcel realized it was too soon but too late because he had fallen in love with the mysterious Abassi.

Abassi lazily sat up. Marcel felt a new coldness cover his body. His eyebrows knitted together as he spoke through his shortness of breath:

"I ... have to go now."

He hurriedly stood up and put his clothes on. He didn't know what time it was, but he still had work that day.

Abassi said nothing. He sat on the stone, staring off into the sky.

"Will I see you again?" Marcel asked.

"No," Abassi said.

He grabbed Abassi's hand, "Why not? Is that what you do? Screw random guys and then never see them again?"

Abassi looked at him.

"Your return will bring no good," Abassi said and then yanked his hand away. Marcel glared at him. If he could, he would've scolded Abassi longer, but time wouldn't allow it. He ran back the way he came to return home.

"Marcel."

Abassi's voice was husky, but instantly Marcel recognized it. The man's fiery fingers stung his flesh. Abassi then ran his fingers down Marcel's back. He stopped when he reached Marcel's plump rear. He grabbed the mounds of flesh. He caressed the cheeks and then roughly spread them apart. His thick cock appeared from under his loincloth. He rammed it up the tight hole and Marcel fiercely cried out.

"Marcel," Abassi said.

"Marcel. Marcel. Hey, Marcel?"

His name was repeated again and again. When he turned his head to answer the call, his face met with his disgruntled manager. Marcel looked around. There was no Abassi, just a computer screen in his direction and a messy fake plant.

"I'm not paying you to daydream. Get back to work."

Marcel didn't know how long he was lost in a daydream or how long the manager had been standing over him, but he hurried back to fixing the computer. Everything just seemed so real.

"Sorry," Marcel said.

"It's because you're up all night playing those video games or whatever. And what happened to your glasses?"

"Someone told me that my glasses cover up my beauty," Marcel said staring off as if he were looking at the memory of last night and then he turned toward his boss.

"You better be able to see without your glasses," his boss muttered and then shook his head. He went back into his office. Marcel sighed. He massaged his face with his hands. He was exhausted. He would've taken the day off, but he needed the money.

"Abassi," he whispered the name so low, his voice was barely audible. He went outside in an attempt to clear his head. His mind was a collage of Abassi. It was as if he were addicted to that strong black man. A sadness wrapped around his heart. It pounded in his chest at just the thought. He had to see him again. It was too difficult to rebuke the urge. At this rate, he wasn't even thinking rationally. This strong yearning controlled him. Did Abassi really think after that passionate dance Marcel would stay away? Even though Abassi said his return would bring no good that wasn't enough to control Marcel's desire.

Marcel rushed home. It was about midnight. His guilt was breathing down his neck like a thousand fingers tugging on him, but it wasn't enough to compete with his desires. His quick footsteps furrowed the grass as he approached the thicket where he and Abassi once stood. He paused. His jagged wheezing quieted the crickets. All the bushes looked the same. Which one camouflaged the portal that connected the worlds? He wasn't wearing his glasses. Everything far away appeared as a blur. Battling the bushes, when he least expected, a whirlwind yanked him through the leaves and into Abassi's world.

It wasn't until he landed on his back, releasing an oomph sound and looked up at the sky that he realized how blinded his impulsive desire was. He wasn't that familiar with the place, and this time he didn't have Abassi as a guide. Besides, how could he face Abassi after disobeying him? It was too late to panic.

What have I done?

The words passed through his mind. He should've returned home, but he came too far to just turn around and go back. The place seemed so much scarier without Abassi around. The stinging silence crept around him. He stood there, taking in the land. An oceanic feeling spread throughout his body. It was impossible to overcome this jungle maze. He took a step further. Before he knew it, he reached new ground with smoke signals rising in the sky. He looked around. There was a tiny path hidden by branches. Marcel stepped over the branches. In the distance he saw the blurry image of a small village. He squinted. Then he noticed a small girl staring at him. How long had she been there?

She wore a sheep skin dress and held a stick in one hand. Her eyes were large and glued on Marcel.

"Hi," he said. He then smiled and leveled himself with her, "By any chance can you tell me where I can find Abassi?"

The wide-eyed girl paused.

"You're funny looking," she said and then giggled.

Marcel gave a crochet smile.

18

"Can you help me?" Marcel pushed on.

"My mommy knows. She knows everything," she said as she flounced her arms about.

Marcel followed her into the village. Buried within the small village was a cottage made of coble stone. Marcel stood outside of the wooden door. The girl kicked the door. She turned to Marcel with a grin, "My mommy can't hear the door unless I hit it. Hit it hard."

When the door opened, a woman appeared in a wine colored dress that circled her ankles.

"Malunda, what have I told you about kicking the door? You tap it lightly," she said and then she noticed Marcel standing behind the girl.

She looked at him and swung her arms around Malunda, "Who are you?"

Her disgruntled face startled Marcel. He waved his hands up.

"Sorry, I was lost and um … I needed help."

She looked him up and down, "Those clothes, that accent … why did you come here?"

"Um … I'm from …"

"Show me your marking," she interrupted.

"Marking …?" Marcel paused. He remembered that tattoo he saw on Abassi's arm.

"You're an outsider," the woman said and then slammed the door in Marcel's face. The baffled Marcel backed up. He was never going to find Abassi. Before he knew it, word got around the village about him – the outsider. He found himself circled by whispers and the focus of hidden eyes.

"There's the outsider. Get him."

Marcel turned around when he heard the violent voice. He was face-to-face with a spear. Blood-thirsty men with eager spears surrounded him. The sharp blades were aimed at every side of his body. The men were dark and muscular. One man spoke:

"What's your reason for coming? Where are the rest of your men?"

"N-no. I don't have any men. Just please – understand. I come from another world."

"Shut your mouth," the soldier growled. Then Marcel's right eye witnessed the flashing movement of a jagged fist blinding him for a moment. The stinging of blackness released tiny shards of light in his vision. His entire face soaked up the pain. Marcel fell backward. While he trembled in pain, he pressed his hand against his eye.

"What is all this commotion?"

Marcel recognized the deep voice. He hurriedly opened his good eye and attempted to open the other. Excitement ripped through Marcel's body. Abassi's shadow covered him, and a sharp pain buzzed in his stomach. He stared into Abassi's beady eyes.

"Abassi," he cried out.

The other man turned to Abassi, "You know this – this outsider?" he nudged Abassi with his elbow. Abassi glared at the man and then turned back to the injured Marcel. Abassi's glare hung heavily above him. Fear rushed through his body; he became overwhelmed by emotion as his heart slammed against his chest. His fingers gripped the dirt. Abassi's face was still like stone. His lips were a straight line. At first he said nothing. He was a statue. The atmosphere was enflamed. Marcel held his breath as Abassi's face twisted in disgust.

"I've never seen this man before," he said, "Take him to the dungeon."

Abassi turned his back and walked away. Marcel wanted to cry out – say anything, but he was voiceless.

Abassi.

The name paused in his mind. This man who had captured his heart, the warm passionate dance – how could he be so cold? He could see lips moving but every sound disappeared. All the emotion drained from Marcel as his body lay limp and his world faded to darkness.

Marcel wasn't sure if it were his imagination or not. He felt Abassi's presence. The light from the opening door engulfed his body. The ropes bit into his wrists. He was lying on the stone floor of the dungeon. The place reeked of dirt and death. A gloom filled the air and in the corner on the opposite side of Marcel was a skull entangled in white hair. Marcel was much too weak to even murmur Abassi's name. He saw Abassi standing in the doorway. The light followed Abassi as he came closer to him.

Abassi unlocked the steel barred doors. His hot breath stung Marcel's welts. He slid his fingers over Marcel's chest wound.

"I told you not to return," he said. His voice was a whisper. Marcel closed his eyes. His body ached, but Abassi's touch was soothing. A tiny whimper escaped his mouth.

"Seeing you merciless is quite the turn on."

Abassi licked his lips and then dragged his tongue over the wound. He felt Marcel's body grow tense. He then rolled his tongue over Marcel's nipples, coating them in saliva.

"You like that?" he said while teasing the sensitive buds with his thumb and finger. He toyed with both nipples, pulling and pinching them until they were hard and sore. Marcel wiggled his restrained wrists from the sensation, but that only made the ropes squeeze him more. He then caressed Marcel's skin with his mouth. Marcel's cock throbbed for attention. An aching groan escaped his lips as Abassi massaged him roughly. Abassi shoved Marcel's body against the wall.

An overbearing heat jolted throughout Marcel. He cried out again. At that moment, Marcel wanted nothing more but to feel Abassi consume him.

"Take me," Marcel struggled to say when their lips parted.

His low voice vibrated on Abassi's chest. Abassi positioned Marcel's legs far apart, revealing every aspect of the man. Abassi then slipped his hand around Marcel's stiff penis. Using his other hand; he inserted one finger into Marcel's hungry hole. A bittersweet yelp pulled from Marcel's throat. He jerked as Abassi dominated him. Abassi stroked the tip of Marcel's cock. His fingers were dampened by tiny beads of pre-cum, falling like raindrops from Marcel. Marcel was begging for a release before Abassi had even used his member on him. Marcel squirmed as another finger pushed into his asshole. Abassi's fingers moved in a scissor-like motion. He didn't hesitate, he knew what Marcel wanted. He removed his fingers and then slipped his cock inside.

Marcel burst into a frenzy of moans as the intruding mass pushed in and out. His voice was harmonized with Abassi's thrusts. He looked away quickly when his eyes met Abassi's passionate stare.

A tiny gasp escaped from Abassi. He thrust in deeply and pulled all the way out. Marcel's greedy hole wanted to keep him inside. He then plunged his man rod back into Marcel. Marcel's toes curled as he cringed from the renew flood of pain mixed with pleasure. Marcel couldn't fetter his climax any longer.

"You like being my plaything, don't you?" Abassi said, but no words came from Marcel, only groans. Abassi didn't wait for an answer; he pushed deep inside the man. Faster and faster, he thrust into the whimpering Marcel. His breaths were heavy. Marcel succumbed to the pleasure. He couldn't hold back any longer. His loins gave in.

His cum decorated Abassi's chest. Abassi gave one last heavy thrust, and in a jagged cry out, his jizz leaked out in globs. The two bodies locked eyes, exchanging small kisses and short breaths. Abassi rested his sweaty broad forehead on Marcel's chest and then wrapped his arms around the delicate man. He paused for a moment. Marcel wished time would never end. Abassi regained his strength and untied Marcel's exhausted wrists.

"We have to leave now."

"B-but I don't want to leave you," Marcel said.

"Are you stupid? You'll die if you stay here any longer," he said.

Marcel then pressed his lips on Abassi's. His arms wrapped around the man's neck.

"Please. I love you," Marcel said with pain decreasing his voice. The two basked in each other's arms, feeling the radiating warmth between them. Marcel knew his fate was too grave; but he couldn't leave Abassi.

"I have to get you out of here," Abassi said in a low murmur.

Marcel could barely hear over his loud breaths.

When Marcel looked up in the entrance of the doorway, his heart fell to the ground. There stood a gawking soldier inflated with shock. He knew this was it. The light enveloped the two like a halo.

"I'm taking him," Abassi said as he walked toward the blood-thirsty soldier in the doorway. Marcel gave Abassi a cautious look, but Abassi looked back at him with smiling eyes.

"Liar. You betray us, chief," the soldier said, "You do know this outsider. You brought him to the village, didn't you? Answer me."

"If you so much share any word about this to the king, I'll kill you myself," Abassi interrupted.

The solider attempted to strike Abassi with his fist. Abassi caught the man's hand. His strength made the soldier's arm tremble. A mask of fear landed over the solider. He backed up. Abassi then released his hand.

23

"I'll make sure you're exiled for this," he said and then ran down the corridor screaming. Abassi took a sharp breath. He stepped back into the dungeon. He reached his hand out to the shuddering Marcel.

"I wanna go home. Abassi. Please take me home."

He clung to Abassi. The two only had minutes to escape. Gripping Marcel's hand, he yanked the weak man off the floor.

"Seeing you naked makes me want to take you right here," Abassi teased.

"How can you say that at a time like this?" Marcel protested.

For a moment, he thought he saw a glimmer of sadness in Abassi's eyes.

"What's going to happen to you? I'm sorry," Marcel said.

"We have no time for apologies."

Going up the stairs was the only way out of the dungeon. When Abassi opened the door to the upstairs, he wasn't surprised. Soldiers with spears bombarded them.

"Put your hand ups," a soldier said.

The cool air wrapped around Marcel as the soldiers lead him and Abassi outside. The spears restrained them. Marcel looked over at Abassi who remained calm.

"Chief Abassi, how dare you bring shame on us," a soldier said.

The soldier then raised his spear at Marcel. Marcel froze in shock. He thrust the weapon forward. Marcel's face reflected off the blade that was about to strike him. Marcel closed his eyes. This was it. Any second, he'd be dead. Stale air consumed him for the moment, and when he grew impatient with anxiety, he witnessed it. Abassi had sacrificed himself. Marcel gasped, and then his voice ripped out of him like a crack of thunder.

"Abassi. Oh my god. Abassi."

He uncontrollably reached his arms out to hold the man, but the wounded Abassi rejected him. He shoved Marcel away.

"Run. Get out of here," he struggled to say.

All the soldiers erupted in an uproar. Marcel didn't want to run away. He couldn't leave Abassi, but he had no time to dwell on the situation either. Marcel burst through the violent crowd. Tears ran down Marcel's face as he squinted and looked forward, never forgetting the last image of the strong Abassi.

Many days passed. Marcel lay awake in bed. He no longer dreamt of Abassi. He didn't dream of anything. He stared at the blurry ceiling. He at least wanted to apologize to him. He looked at the bruises on his wrists.

The startling doorbell shook his mind. He put his glasses on and approached the door. He took a breath. Who could it be? This late? His fingers wrapped around the doorknob as he eased the door open, assuming it was the lady from the first floor.

His mouth quivered. He wanted to speak but nothing came out. Abassi stared back at him. His body was covered in blood stained wounds.

"Abassi. I never thought I'd see you again."

Abassi smirked.

"They cover up your beauty," he said and then slid Marcel's glasses off. A strong relief pooled in Marcel's chest as their eyes locked once again. He imagined he would have more to say. He even spent days thinking about his reaction, but the two just stood there. Whether it was shock or happiness, Marcel felt paralyzed. Then Abassi gently pinched his arm to reassure him, it wasn't a dream.

IT'S NOT DIGIORNO
By Kels Brecter

Kels lives in Salt Lake City Utah where he works for himself as a freelance writer and a personal organizer. His favorite color is buffet.

"Get me another beer," he said. And I did.

"Get me another slice of pie," he said. And I did, with a clean fork, clean plate, and scoop of vanilla ice cream on the side.

"Get me..."

"Get me..."

"Get me..."

And I did, every time. He sat on the living room sofa playing video games, some new one I bought for him that he picked out. I sat at the kitchen table working on my quarterly reports.

The game ended and he turned off the television before climbing on the table, his feet at the edge, facing me. I sat in the chair, looking up at the smirk on his face. *What nationality is he?* I wondered. When he applied for a job over six months ago he checked other on the application.

His smirk turned to a big smile. He unzipped, whipped it out, and whizzed all over my head.

# # # # #

After graduating with a degree in business management, I opened a pizza joint just off campus. It turned into a gold mine for me, and I have been doing it for twenty years. That's all I serve is pizza, three different kinds; pepperoni, cheese, or ham and pineapple. You can add a 12 oz. bottle of Coke or Dr. Pepper from the cooler for two bucks

27

more, but that's it. I sell it by the slice during lunch and it gets busy as hell as students rush in between classes. In the evening, you can order the whole pizza because at night, they come in with friends to unwind and do homework. The place is small, has one pool table and one pinball machine. It's kind of old school I know, but it brings them in.

Not only do college students eat my food, but also they work for me, and I have a high turnover of employees coming and going, it's like they change jobs with every semester or degree change. He started working for me in the fall; is he Asian? He came to the states from Australia to attend school and applied to work at the restaurant. He was a good worker, always on time and did his job well; that's all I knew about him.

That is until the incident at the kitchen table. Now I could tell you that he is uncut, perhaps not the biggest, but I imagined it would slide nicely down my throat if ever given the chance to make it grow.

I'm not even sure how he found out where I live. *Did he follow me?* He just showed up at my door late one night. I was already in my boxers brushing my teeth. "Delivery," he said, pizza in hand when I answered the door in my robe. "I added a new special sauce to it, I hope you like it." Even though it did have a different taste, it was still my pizza in the box, but since I don't offer delivery he got the box from somewhere else.

From then on, he just started showing up on a regular basis, usually weekends. We would play video games, (which I hate) watch a movie, or I would help him with his homework. Actually, helping him with his homework usually turned into doing it for him. Then he would fall asleep on my sofa while I went to bed. Maybe he is Blatino.

Spring break started just like any other of his visits. He showed up, I made dinner, did the dishes and we hung out.

But on that particular visit he whizzed on me. *What the fuck? Where did that come from?* He shook off the last few drops on my reports then zipped up and went to bed in my room. I slept on the sofa.

# # # # #

"What's for breakfast?" he asked the next morning, waking me from my sleep, a kink in my neck. I fixed him a breakfast burrito with sausage, eggs, cheese and sour cream with a cup of coffee. After cleaning up, I went shopping for more beer and groceries. I didn't have much in the house, and I needed to buy something good to eat. One time I made him a peanut butter and jelly sandwich and he responded, "What's this? PB&J? If I wanted poor boy college food, I'd spend the weekend at my apartment."

When I returned home from the grocery store, I found him in the back yard, stretched out on a Chaise lounge, nothing on but green shorts that hung to his knees. It was a different look than his usual attire; a pair of Chinos or Bonobos with a Cardigan or Blazer, a bow tie, and sometimes dark rimmed glasses just for show. He always dressed sharp, but now he was nearly naked, arms behind his head soaking in the sun even though he did not need any. His body was dark tan, so beautiful, like a teenage body so often is. Noticeably sexy, slender, and yet finely muscled. He had to be a mix of Latino and Asian, or so I thought.

"Go ahead," he said, and I wondered what he meant. My mind racing with what I wanted to do to do him, my eyes darting all over his body, wondering where to begin. "Lick 'em," he said. Again, I wondered what he meant; there was not an inch of him I would not lick. *Maybe he does not care where I begin, or maybe he is playing a prank on me.*

My body trembling, I knelt beside him, slowly stuck out my tongue and slid the tip through the hair beneath his arms. He didn't move, so I did it again, and again, lapping up his scent and soaking his under arm.

Still shaking, I moved to the other side and did the same thing, intoxicated by the taste; soaking his under arm with my tongue, over and over again. My tongue moved slowly toward his nipple.

29

"Times up," he said, moving toward the house. "Come on, we're going to be late for work."

"Yes sir," I said standing, knees trembling. Wait a minute, when did I start calling him sir? He works for me, and I'm probably old enough to be his father.

Business was slow, as it always is during spring break. I probably would not have even gone in to work if he did not say anything. I would rather have stayed home in the back yard on my knees, my face buried in his pits the entire day.

There were only three of us working the joint, Jessica came in to work the register while he made the pizzas and flirted with her. He would come up behind her and whisper in her ear then the two of them would giggle, often looking in my direction, then she would blush.

"Would you like to come over?" he asked her as we were cleaning up. With it being so slow, I wasn't even going to bother staying open for dinner, but when he invited her over I wished I would have stayed open.

After cooking them dinner, a sweet and sour chicken stir fry over rice, I cleaned up and did the dishes while they sat on the sofa. They weren't doing much sitting though, he was really making the moves on her, and she wasn't even trying to push him away. But then neither would I if I were she.

As I was rummaging through the fridge, looking for the cheese cake, he came up behind me, startling me, and whispered in my ear as he pressed up against me. "Where do you keep your condoms?"

# # # # #

After she left, he wanted to take a bath, so I ran the water for him, adding lots of bubbles. Once the tub was full, he told me to leave the bathroom.

While he soaked, I tried to find his scent on the bed sheets but could only find hers, so I put them in the wash. Thinking I had some time alone, I rushed to the waste basket in my room and found the used condom, I turned it inside out, closed my eyes and got a whiff of him; and my first taste.

He started yelling for me and for a moment I thought I was busted, but then I realized he was still in the tub, and I ran to him.

"Wash my back," he said sitting up in the tub. For a moment, I cursed myself for adding so many bubbles, I wanted to look into the water and get a better look. But, his wet hair stuck to his head and hung in his eyes, adding to his sultry look.

After rubbing his back with a bar of soap, he handed me the bottle of shampoo, and I lathered up his hair, and then used a paper cup from under the sink to rinse it out.

He lay back down in the tub, and instinctively I started rubbing his chest, now grateful for the bubbles, they made his skin silky smooth, my hand gliding ever so softly over his chest and torso. Since I knew he had an orgasm not to long before, I resisted going any lower than that, my hand stopped at his pubes then back up to his chest.

He stood in the tub, and I reached for the towel, drying him off. He walked to my bed, naked, giving me a second look at his ass.

The first time I saw his naked ass was when I watched him through the crack he left open in my door, her legs wide open, and his body filling the gap, his ass bouncing up and down, muscle flexing with every downward thrust. I wished it were my legs that were wrapped around him.

He climbed into bed, and I pulled the blanket up over him, turned off the light and went downstairs.

We went to the restaurant early the next day, and I called Jessica, telling her not to come in the rest of the week. It was slow enough for him and me to run it on our own.

Two days later, spring break was nearly over, and he would be back in school, only coming over on weekends, and that's only if he had nothing better to do.

The time passed quickly. Make breakfast, go to work, come home, make dinner, clean up, play video games, go to bed.

Then on Sunday, the morning before all the students were to arrive back, the dishwasher broke. Being in the restaurant business, I had gotten pretty handy with those kinds of things and could fix it myself.

I took the front panel off the washer and saw the problem, and asked him to go downstairs and get some tools. I asked him again, then went downstairs and got them myself. When I came back up, he was leaning on the counter next to the washer. The entire time that I was cleaning out the clogged hose on the washer, his crotch was inches from my face. I wanted to unclog his hose while I was down there. When I stood back up his shirt was off.

"Did I say you could stand up Bitch?" I got back down on my knees, his crotch inches from my face. "Take them off." And I did. I popped open the buttons on his shorts, slid my fingers in his boxers and pulled them both down in one swoop.

He leaned against the counter, dick standing up, and a flush of heat entered my belly. Is he going to let me? I waited for the command. Nothing. He turned around, leaned his elbows on the counter. Again, my eager mouth waited for the command. He farted, and he found it hugely amusing. Still though I waited for his command, thinking he would ask me to dive in with my tongue for no other reason than a good laugh.

When he regained his composure, he turned back around to face me, his dick was still standing. Throbbing. He needed release, bad. I no longer waited for his command and leaned in. The scent of his unwashed dick filled my nostrils, my mouth opened, tongue out, a drip of drool on the corner of my mouth.

"What the fuck are you doing?" he shouted, stopping me, a mere centimeter from pure pleasure. My gut ached.

He took my belt and tied it around my wrists behind me, found a piece of rope in my tool box and tied one end around the belt and the other end around a post in my kitchen. When I first bought the house the first thing I did was knock out the wall between the kitchen and the living room to open it up. I put in a post from the floor to the ceiling to act as a support beam. It worked out nice having it open because it allowed me to spy on him when I was in the kitchen.

His dick remained solid during the entire process of tying me up. "Some guys just can't be trusted," he said standing back in front of me. "I can take care of it myself." And he did, keeping just out of my reach.

The cum got in my hair, up my nose, and ran down my neck. I stuck out my tongue like a kid in falling snow and managed to catch a few drops.

When he was done, he went upstairs and showered. Coming back into the kitchen, dressed for work, he filled a bowl with water and sat it on the floor next to me, then left, taking my keys and my car.

Six hours later, when he returned, he fed me a slice of pizza. I took one bite and immediately made a connection between him and the special sauce baked into the melted cheese.

THE ITALIAN SLOB
R. Talent

> *R. Talent is a homoerotic writer with one hand on the keyboard and another always down his pants.*

"Look at ol' Priscilla Pumpernickel dressed so fuckin' pretty in her pink lace," woofed Ralph Waldo Donavon, a jolly redheaded redneck with girth, pulling proudly on the straps of his dirty overalls.

It was a crude sight to behold. Both utterly disgusting as it was cock-throbbing arousing, standing back there in those dark mountainous woods by the fleeing moonlight. There was a small measure of me that wanted to turn away from this horrific scene, sensing something bad was on the bend. Yet, the part I was driven by, kept my feet planted firmly on the Tennessee soil with this scandalous curiosity itching away at me, wanting to see the end part of our plan coming to its complete close.

"Whee-wee Priscilla Pumpernickel shol' is a purrr-dy doll," crooned David Oliver, a gargantuan black man with a gruff reddish-brown beard, using his crumple southern draw to make reference to the local tramp that was strangled to death of a hefty wad of his half-brother Albert's sweet mulatto jizz.

The four other guys standing about continued to laugh heartedly surrounding this odd being slowly coming to with a pair of thick hairy arms tied behind his back.

"F-U-fuckin' pretty I tell you!" David repeated, stomping his large heavy boot at the captive's platinum blond wig, creating another round of hard mirth amongst the bearish men. "F-U-fuckin' pretty!"

# # # # #

The months leading up to this final showdown had been a longtime coming between our quiet mountain town of Kingsfordland,

35

Tennessee, and the defects from the premier Irish and Italians families that once littered New England.

By then, around the mid- to late 40s, it wasn't all that uncommon for a disgraced mobster to make a side step through the Great Appalachians on his way down to Florida. At the time, this was believed to be the most intelligent way for them to stay out of dodge of their starch-stuffed colleagues waiting along the Eastern Seaboard to whack them off. It was suspected that if they were lucky enough to sneak by without notice that they would be lucky enough to hop a boat over to Cuba to make it with Havana girls or over to the Bahamas to start a new, more fanciful life.

When these ruffians first started trickling in a few decades earlier, we were very leery of these outsides being small town folks like we were. In particular, these smooth-talking city slickers with their gravely accents who thought they were superior to us. While we remained a unified group not so fond of change, some of the rebellious womenfolk were dazzled by their gun-blazing bravado and their wild style of dress that often made our Sunday's best look like Thursday's slops. We were outraged when widespread rumors suggested that some of the boys in neighboring towns were being forced to raise their abandoned offspring as their own pride. But after the dust settled, we found that none of them meant us any harm. So we decided from then on to let bygones be bygones and be done with it.

Of course that was before this scrawny little Italian shit face named Lollo Aurelie came kicking up dirt through the dusty streets of Kingsfordland, bloody and bruised on blazing Tuesday afternoon.

We should've known then that the goddamn son of a bitch was up to no good, lying to us that he tripped and fell a few times trying to outrun a big ol' grizzly. Looking at his ruined dapper suit, Tully suggested that somebody elsewhere in the mountains roughed up the boy since dress clothes weren't usually made to frolic in the woods. But seeing that we were a hospitable bunch, some of the locals took to cleaning him up and seeing after him like he was one of our native sons.

Unlike others that were more than eager to knock off the dust and get going, the five-foot-eight beanpole began planting roots. Renting a room near town and getting a job at the post office because he could read and write and use one of those typewriters so well. He fitted in so well that it was like he had always been there. We were even warming up to the idea of him going steady with one of the prettiest girls on our side of the state. Everything was hunky-dory for the first couple of months before certain "tensions" started to arise. It took a while but when we got to the bottom of it after we were able to put the pieces of the puzzle together.

When Aurelie was in the company of an all-white crowd, he couldn't stop himself from appealing to the hardcore racists. Suggesting that most of the black folks thought they were running the show in Kingsfordland since they owned the most land around there. But when he got around an all-black crowd, he addressed everyone as his brother and sister, explaining that Italy was just a stone's throw away from Africa, all the while calling every white man and woman out of their name.

For the time, it may not have seemed like a very big deal for the segregated South. And while Tennessee wasn't any different from any state in the union in its brand of hate, our remote neck of the woods was too small for the blacks and the whites not to get along. We were bright enough to know that we needed each other desperately if we were going to make a decent profit off our greatest commodity – moonshine.

So when he learned that his mouth had got him in a lot of hot water, Aurelie called some of his other mob defects to swarm our little mountain town. While Aurelie may have not gotten his hands on our moonshine, his goons made sure that they got their hands on our town. Strong-arming the local businesses for so-called protection – protection from them, that is. And when certain business folks didn't obey the new rules, Aurelie, the self-appointed boss of the whole operation, started ordering his men to attack some of the same people that helped him get settled in. Some he even made victims to brutal defilement, regardless of gender, as a way to humiliate others with his newfound power. I guess he figured that if he couldn't swim with the Big Fish up north, he would go for a much smaller pond down south. Being that this had always been home to the bunch of us, we quietly stood our ground thinking of some new ways of chasing those sorry bastards out of town. We soon got word back that some of those powerful crime families had put such a high bounty on the heads of those untrustworthy souls that we got the big idea of making our small town the French Rivera of the South based on the amount of money we thought we could head. Cool heads prevailed noting that making deals with those devils meant them possibly dipping their smelly toes into our moonshine production, and considering how vast it carried throughout those mountains, we would be nothing more than killing the roaches for the rats.

Since we were so far removed from the rest of the known world, we decided to use our curse as our blessing. It took a while to get everybody on the same page. Once we did it was like we were a hungry anteater taking out the ants. We started out being nice and humane about the whole process by blindfolding and kidnapping the ones we thought we could take and dumping them miles out of the way. The worst they were, the further we drove to put them out. Aurelie was no fool. He was hot on our trail from the very beginning. We were just smart enough to hide behind the corner quick enough for him and his protection not to spot us. We quickly had to shift gears a little when the old routine wasn't working anymore. Because those goons were always on the hunt for our moonshine, we took to the art of persuasion. Offering them a sample of our product with the promise of getting them an in. We grew up on moonshine, so it's like blood in our veins. To a city slicker who often hails it as this mystical drink that their lips rarely touch, we knew that it wouldn't take much to knock their lights out. So we chose to scare off those who were smart enough to leave and killing off those that was dumb enough to stick around.

After we gave Auerlie's right-hand man a one-way ticket over a steep ridge, Aurelie was fair game, and we were in for the kill.

By then, it was well known that Aurelie couldn't satisfy his hunger for exceptionally beautiful women. So much so he was importing them from as far away as Wisconsin to satisfy his animalistic lust. As a result, the whole town chipped in to hire one of the prettiest whores around to offer Aurelie a drink of Tennessee mountain moonshine in her boudoir. He was barely undressed when we stormed the room to find him passed out on the bed with an Irish toothache still raging on in his comatose state. Before the five of us could send the bastard back to hell where he came from, Ralph looked over at the prostitute's belongings and asked to have a minute with Aurelie. He later followed up by asking us to meet him in our usual spot in the woods an hour later.

"You're not going to leave this son of a bitch like this, now are you?" I asked, looking at the end result after finding the gumption to ask such a daring question through the dying laughter in the wooded mountains that night.

It was hard to really look down at the almighty Lollo Aurelie, flat on his sorry Italian back, barely recognized through the piles of harlot paint splattered across his rugged face. That is except for his unique aquiline nose. There he was, a man who groomed himself to be one of the most powerful monsters we had ever seen, only to be humiliated like a bitch in heat in a ripped pink blouse and some lace pink stockings.

No bottom. Only everything else he naturally came into this world with.

"Yeah, doggie," Ralph offered excitedly, bouncing in his squat position between the pair of slender hairy legs roped at the ankles to the sturdy branches about. "But not a minute shy before all have a little fun pumpin' ol' Priscilla's nickel. It'll be rude not to after she got all dolled up for us!"

Ralph laughed some more, taking his dirty middle finger and shoving it into the open jar slimy bacon fat at his foot. He then goes onto pull it out of there and shoved it into the puckered poop chute jutting out at him.

Aurelie gave a mild groan of consciousness from his drunken stupor, almost acknowledging to the rest of us that he was still there, still present in his swimming mind. But knowing the way of the distilled whiskey, at best he was still drifting through dreamland, indifferent to the consensual rape.

After Ralph took his stubby long finer out of the wrinkled hollow, Ralph reached over and smeared it across Aurelie's prettily made-up face.

"Priscilla never looked so damn purdy." David grinned down at the runny makeup, tugging at his hungry crotch ready to feast.

The words were there. Perverse in their barbaric need to strip away the last piece of dignity that Aurelie tried his best to hold onto. It was disturbing as it was disgusting to watch the rest of his manhood being taken away. Even I felt sorry for the cruel bastard. Still though, though the deliverance of David Oliver's last words, there was the confirmation and shock over what was to become of Lollo Aurelie that caused my hambone to stir.

Before I could determine if this newest revelation was decent or corrupt, Ralph undid the top of his overalls and took to his knees in front of Aurelie, making him naked from the waist down.

Without question, that left very little doubt to those standing about to guess what was going to happen next, with Ralph glazing his squat piece of sausage meat with the available bacon grease.

At this point, I was driven made with lust in vicious anticipation of what was to come when this ounce of human compassion came flooding back through my veins. My eyes were on Ralph finger-poking Aurelie, but I also saw David over there out of the corner of my eye changing his position over there near Aurelie's head. Instead of facing out towards Aurelie's feet, David was looking down at Aurelie. But I really caught wind of what was about to go down when David used his boots to steady himself on the covered parts of Aurelie's arm and pulled his tree trunk of a black root cock out of his denims.

Nobody, not even the law, was bold enough to tell David Oliver what he could and could not do. But even if we thought we could that night, the rancid piss coming out of that incredibly large hose was flowing so fast and furious directly into Aurelie's face that all that was left for any of us to do was give off a concerned sigh while David heaved out a relieving groan. We were left baffled when Aurelie stopped fighting his bath and opened his mouth to the wild stream foaming in his mouth.

"I swear if I didn't know any better," David commented, putting his cock back in his pants. "I would think ol' Priscilla got off on that nasty shit!"

"Don't you know that good ol' Priscilla will let any man do any damn thing to her purdy self?" Ralph coolly hooted.

"She's a fuckin' nymph!"

I looked over at David looking over his huge shoulder back at pudgy Ralph who was raring to go with his flared mushroom head banging at Aurelie's lubed backdoor.

Piss was still dripping hot off of Aurelie's face when I saw that the inevitable was imminent as Ralph cautiously peeled back the tight foreskin of his sweet pickled pecker and nuzzled the end tip between that trembling cleft.

"Aggghhhh!" Aurelie gasped hazily, letting out a long sigh that grew into an ugly grunt the more Ralph used his knees to grip a better grip on the dirt.

Aurelie tensed up several times during the initial invasion, even bucking back a few times without a clear intent of blessing or rebuff.

"Listen to that purdy piggy squeal her sweet melody!" Ralph proclaimed to the moonlight, sinking his sticky pecker in as far as it would go in the poor cunt. Ralph held steady with Aurelie letting out a girlish shrill to the surrounding mountains and molehills to let them know that he was still in his body, as if he began to grasp that he was helpless in what was happening.

Ralph lifted up his dirty tee shirt and pulled it back behind his neck. "Now it's time to really poke Ms. Piggy!"

Ralph got into a real comfortable position that allowed him to really start fucking Aurelie. It was an amazing sight to behold. Ralph was a fat son of a bitch that usually gave out of breath just by getting out of his rocking chair. But that night Ralph worked, working up a steady sweat putting the screws to that exhausted pipe. He was working harder than I had ever seen him work before, with Aurelie reaping all the benefits against the steady pounding.

I knew that Aurelie wasn't really there when he kept on looking for where his own screams were coming from, fighting hard to come to more than anything else, silently looking around for a helping hand.

"Yeah, get that sorry bitch, Ralphie!" Malcolm, biracial kin to both Ralph and David, cheered on.

"I'm getting it in Cousin Mal! I'm getting it in!" Ralph huffed.

Ralph held steady sawing away at Aurelie grunting and groaning heatedly before he pulled his pecker all the way out and crammed it all the way back in to get the most grumbling out of the womanized man.

"Oh God," Aurelie screeched, still looking elsewhere for the author of his straggled voice.

With sweat just pouring off him, Ralph plunged deeper into Aurelie, stopped cold, threw his head back to the humid night sky, and howled an obscene deposit into that sweet hole that violent pushed him out.

Ralph barely got his wind after the great white drainage before hairy Clyde, one of the other guys standing about, knocked the redneck flat on his caboose and quickly mounted the Italian Stallion like an Italian Mare with absolutely no fuss.

Clyde pounded Aurelie out with his curved knob for another ten minute strong before he too emptied out his trash.

Malcolm took Clyde out in the same fashion Clyde did Ralph with the major difference being that Malcolm looked the most comfortable between those open pair of legs.

Fifteen minutes later, Malcolm pulled his furious baby maker out of the naked abyss that was quivering to push out the collective cream of all three men from his loosened crack.

I walked over behind Aurelie fanatically rotating his powerful hips like he didn't care who was next, letting me and everyone else around know that while he was still relatively out of it, his rosebud was still wholly in the game.

"Billy Boy, I don't know," David noted over my shoulders with me coming out of my trousers for my turn. "Look at that beautiful gaping twat over there just oozing with hot velvety spoo. I mean, I know the good for nothing slut got plenty of round pussy for me to get off on with this huge motherfucker I'm packing, but you're a bit more modest than me. No offense. I don't know if she'll do the trick man. I don't fuckin' know!"

David called himself trying to be coy with his words. He was right. Compared to his Uncle Malcolm with his enormous cock, I was relatively smaller than him even though I had spade over both Ralph and Clyde with my long slender length.

With my manliness on the line, I dropped to my dirty knees and pushed into that slimy pink crack. It was so scrumptiously warm and soft that it felt like walking through a tropical paradise making Aurelie take it down to the furry hilt. It was feeling so good inside that pulsing snatch that I would return the favor by tweaking Aurelie's teasing nipples through the tattered blouse.

Aurelie began to cry out as I pumped into him deep and hard, putting him through both joy and agony rocking every inch I had to give to him. The more aggressive I got, the warmer that hole became mine to take.

"I guess it was plenty of pussy for you, huh, Billy Boy? Wasn't it? Plenty!" David guffawed as I wiped away sweat from my lowly brow.

That sorry son of a bitch was feeling so fuckin' sweet, I nearly forgot where I was or that 'Priscilla' was still a fuckin' man with a small tail between his legs.

"You gonna take my load, Priscilla? Huh, baby? You gonna take my load?" I growled with a new vigor in taking that ass. "I know you are. You know why? 'cause you're the best little whore around, aincha?"

Aurelie incoherently moaned.

I fucked that sweet hole to kingdom come, feeling like my balls were going back into my body smacking against that voluptuous keister.

"C'mon, Priscilla, baby, open up! Open up that pussy for Billy Boy! Ahhh, yeah, that's it! There it is" Oh, fuck, bitch!"

I lost it after that. Cum spewed out of me and joined the already slimy mess I was swimming in as I reminded myself that I was taken out by another man's juicy asshole.

"Oh damn!"

I nearly bowled over to the ground from pure fatigue.

I would've sworn that I was knocked over like the rest of them before me had it not been for David looking me straight in the eye with his long thick black cock sinking into Lollo Aurelie's piss-stained mouth hanging off of the platform.

"Don't you dare bite it, bitch!" David barked.

David hunkered won even further into Aurelie's mouth which from my angel looked like Aurelie was sword-swallowing a lead pipe.

The fact that even in his semi-conscious state Aurelie was able to take much of the surreal flesh down his gullet was quite a remarkable feat. Although I had been on the other end of it a handful of times when David had me to suck him off when his wife was too busy rearing his twelve kids to satisfy him, my paramount was just getting my lips around the enormous head. And there David was over there fucking his mouth like it was meant to be a proper hole.

"Open your fuckin' mouth, cunt! Open that fuckin' mouth!"

I don't' think there was a soul in those woods that couldn't hear Aurelie gurgling with cock rammed down his pretty little throat that night with a loose-hanging pair of balls whacking him in the nostrils with every forceful lunge.

"Priscilla's a happy milk mouth slut." Clyde egged on against a tree, stroking his sleeping log.

"Don't you know that Priscilla Pumpernickel loves playing the peppermint stick?" David added, making me think of his killer brother as he kept on scraping and assaulting the pair of tonsils just below him.

David continued to pump his cock into that waiting mouth. I swore he was doing down to his guts the way Aurelie was choking on it.

Then, without warming, David stuffed his entire shaft down Aurelie's throat and just held it there. I thought the way Aurelie was choking on it David was out to give him death by dick.

Once David pulled up, though, and pulled his cock out of the awaiting mouth, Aurelie erupted with thick spit gushing out of his mouth with chunky wads of slob running down over his eyes with great gasps of air following suit before David rode his face a few minutes more.

"Time to get in some butt," David publicize in childish glee, getting up from his place on Aurelie's worn face.

45

I saw David get up and come towards me, but didn't have a clue that I was actually in his way. I was out of it watching David do his thing and didn't come back to what I was doing until this familiar warmth swathed my trouser snake let me know that I never retreated out of Aurelie.

David quickly replaced me, ruthlessly sliding into home in a smooth stroke while Aurelie yowled like a wounded mutt in pain and outrage. Except this time Aurelie wasn't nearly as groggy as he had been before. Aurelie might've come to while getting his throat reamed, but failed to let the rest of us know. But when David shoved his larger-than-life cock far up his poor stretched-out rectum, Aurelie had no choice but to let the mountains around us know he had sobered up real quick.

"Fuck! I'm no pansy, you filthy motherfucker! I'm a man! I'm a man!" Aurelie cried with the cock tearing him in two.

"Hush up, bitch," David snarled, driving back into him out of malice. "You ain't no fuckin' man wearing some pantyhose!"

"Aggghhhhh!!!" Aurelie moaned and shook with a violently tremor.

"See, what I tell you, Priscilla. You even moan like the no good tramp you are!"

"Stop, please, stop!" Aurelie sputtered with tears and leftover spit covering his eyes.

"Hush up, bitch, or I'll really hush you up!""

David leaned forward and began to hump in sheer earnest. It was quite clear to everyone standing around that David and Aurelie were both desperate for this to be over. The only difference being that David wanted to cum badly when he did. Just not before having some more fun with the son of a bitch by offering him some of the most lethal lashings one bull hung man could ever deliver.

"Huh? You get off on having a real man like me up in your tummy, huh, Priscilla?" David cooed sinisterly against the soft whimpers below him.

"My name is not Priscilla, you ugly fuck!" Aurelie shouted in pain.

David stopped dead in his tracks, raising his huge body up by his hands, and slapped Aurelie across the face followed by a ringing noise that bounced off those tall trees.

"Look, you Italian slob. You'll be what I want you to be, you hear? If I say you're good ol' Priscilla Pumpernickel, you should be quite proud and dandy to be Priscilla for a man like me. Got it you worthless son of a bitch? Good!"

David went back to the beating that hole up, plunging it with no loss of rhythm and stride. Aurelie immediately burst with loud grunts that grew into wolf howls, but that was nothing compared to the slop sounds that his hole was making after loosening its tightened grip around that impossibly large cock.

David hollered against the deafening noise of his wet pounding, "That how you take your man, Priscilla! That's my girl, Ms. Pumpernickel!"

Aurelie shocked us all (or me at least) when I looked down and saw that his corn desperately needed to be shucked, beading with the stuff that he was already stuffed with. He may've been hard all the while the rest of us were fucking the son of a bitch

And the bombshells didn't end there, either. Aurelie began to really get into the action working hard to roll his hips hard back on David to help him get his job done thoroughly. I thought Aurelie might've been more effective had his hands been free to claw at the giant moonshiner's broad back instead of behind his back. I quickly learned otherwise when I saw that the great Lollo Aurelie willingly accept his doable role as the late Priscilla Pumpernickel.

47

The odd tragedy in all of this was that once Aurelie crossed over to Priscilla, David couldn't really enjoy her in the role constantly blubbering that he ruined some of the best pussy in town.

His movement started to change, going from this knife-and-jab motion to this lovey-dovey lovemaking with Aurelie calling David by his name, begging the brute to fuck him like he meant it, make him feel like a real woman.

This was everything David needed to hear, as he soon made the announcement that he was going to shoot.

"Ah, shit! I'm gonna blow this mug! Ahhh!"

David sped up, and once again stopped once he rammed every inch of meat into that bottomless pit and roared like a lion coming inside of that hole.

I thought David was going to die the way he held still over Aurelie with sweat rolling off him and washing the make-up off of the painted Priscilla's purdy face.

Aurelie shook with David underneath him, but seemed to fall into seizures the way David ripped out of him with the loudest pop outside of a severe thunderstorm.

And just like before, David moved quickly back over to Aurelie's mouth and barked, "Clean this shit up so I can take it back to the missus tonight."

# # # # #

No, Kingsfordland didn't have much of a problem out of Lollo Aurelie after that. Though, we sealed his emasculate fate by leaving him out in the middle of the street for the whole town to see him pretty in pink. We thought he would've left running for the hills. But he quietly got up and limped back towards the mountains in the same direction where he originally came.

48

When I got a job with the Census Bureau a couple of years later, I was surprised to learn that David's wife had passed away during childbirth a year earlier, but his new wife looked like a dolled-up Aurelie, though she adamantly insisted her name was Priscilla Oliver, David Oliver's newest housewife.

CALIFORNIA LOVE
R. Talent

"Man, I don't see why we can't have our own crack at this love game," Antonio Barbera, the six-foot-seven former bodyguard of my ex-boyfriend, mouthed.

It was just like a scene out of one of those cheesy chick flicks where we had just darted out of a burst of pouring rain. I happened to be posted up against the stucco wall, and the black Guatemalan was standing in front of me looking as if he had lost some weight smelling of really expensive cologne. He was tugging on the lapels of my fifties style waiter's uniform looking as if he wanted to smother his blubbery lips over mine and wildly carry me off into the sunset. There was a romantic side of me that was truly rooting for him to. Go back east where it all started and start this thing anew. Maybe even dare pick up where I left off like none of this ever happened or before I got caught up in this crazy world. But, the reality was that even though I was far from getting my life back on track, I actually liked my life the way it was right now. Could it stand some improvements? Absolutely. No doubt. It felt good just the same though, as if I was finally breathing again without the constant weight or worry that some well kept secrets could come out.

I just looked into the soul of the giant man in front of me. I couldn't pull my words together, but he knew my thoughts better than I did. And with that, the only thing left for me to do was stand on my tiptoes to reach up and kiss the clean cut man before darting back out into the rain toward my car.

# # # # #

It was my fault really. I went straight to the top with no brakes. So there was no other choice but for me to fall back to the ground. I can't cry over too much spilled milk, though. My descent wasn't hard. The ride was sweet while it lasted. I got to live a baller lifestyle beyond my wildest dreams for a little while, long enough to get use to the ins and outs and left it all behind with a nice parting gift.

The rollercoaster ride for this event began a few years back when I reconnected with a childhood friend. He was a singer who never made it, big who was on a record label with a legendary rapper named Cyclone who was still making moves in the game. Long story short – after Mathis and I caught Cyclone in concert – we headed back to get down, and it exploded into an all-out orgy with the burly immigrant bodybuilder being the first to pluck this wonderful ass, followed by the star attraction and the rest of his well-endowed entourage.

The story should've ended there. It should've been one of those once-in-a-lifetime encounters for everybody to jack off to later in their alone time. And, that was exactly what it was for a while. It slowly grew into something more when one-by-one these men came back into town and wanted to know if I had some free time in my schedule to meet up with them. I can't say that there wasn't a time that I didn't pencil them in somewhere. I was very much interested in recreating some of the action we experienced from that night. With an enormous smile on my face, I can't say that any of those men feel short of my expectations. In fact, a few of them got it so well that I felt the only way I could ever be so sated again was if I took on their whole crew just one more time. Not long afterwards, I began to receive special request to fly out for the weekend to join some of these men before I became a regular in their circle and never went back home.

I was sort of lost as to where to find my place in this new world. I was still more comfortable wearing regular clothes instead of looking as if I just stepped out of a music video. I couldn't go incognito around the crew because it was well known that I had slept with just about everybody and then some, even reducing myself to giving hand jobs under the table. I quickly found my real place when it became routine for me to help take care of some of the guys who struck out with some of the girls at that club. I think after a while a few of them enjoyed my services so much that a few of them didn't even bother to spit game so busy trying to lure me into the dark bathroom for a slow blowjob or a quick shot of ass. I didn't mind. I was ashamed of being a freak for dick like that. Especially, when we were doing it in ways where we were always this close to getting caught.

I was starting to get off on how many ways I could get these guys off in a day when the guys started slacking off in sheets. I could tell in their crotches that they still really wanted to do something, but something or someone was baller-blocking them altogether. The picture became crystal clear when I was summoned up to a hotel suite where I found Cyclone and his biscuit-brown sheen spread out naked on the bed.

Anyone listening to the suggestive lyrics of the legendary rapper would easily walk away believing that he was one of the biggest players around. Why wouldn't he be? He was a very attractive, muscled-down, tatted up, well-known and well-liked brotha in the music industry with money galore. His only faux pas was that thing between his legs. He had an extremely big dick – like freak show circus big – dick so big that it could've really been a third leg with its own fleshly sock torn at the toe. He couldn't just pull it out without someone crying rape and threatening to take his fortune. It was why he had his boys run a train on me that night at the hotel, to open me up good to take him. He knew that I could take him because of that. He knew I was one of those freaks that would go that extra mile to milk that pipe so good that it would take him a day or two just to recover. So I did.

What I wasn't expecting was that I would spend the next five years of my life doing just that. Wherever he was, I wasn't too far behind keeping the bed warm. It wasn't exclusive, of course. I knew he had to be seen with an ocean of beautiful women to keep up appearances. I wasn't put on a leash. I was encouraged to do the same seeing that I was seen as part of the entourage, and everybody seemed to have a girlfriend or a wife on the side to lay claim to. That was my plan, too. It just got derailed when I let my emotions get caught up with the man behind the glitzy persona. The bedroom was quite nice, but the other rooms around the house suited us just fine as well. I guess that was where the battle was lost. I forgot to keep the chase going. I forgot the freedom that spontaneous sex with other men brought about. It became all about him all the time. I think he began to feel the same way about me, too.

So imagine my disbelieve when after an afternoon of marathon sex he announced that he was getting married to this French chick he met six months earlier when we were celebrating our anniversary over in St. Tropez. He told me that he wanted to settle down and have a family. I could've been cool with that, very understanding, if he just shut his mouth right there. No. He decided to tell me that this chick was the one because she had an oversized vagina that could easily fit him like a glove. Like I was just some damn sleeve he could fit into. If I thought I was mad before, I was more than livid than ever when he asked me if I would mind being one of the groomsmen at his wedding.

I just lost it. I went from crying like a little bitch and taking the liquor bottle to the head spending the entire weekend draining his bodyguard with abandonment issues of all of his bodily fluids. Antonio swore he was in love with me after the ordeal. I tried telling myself I felt something for him, too, but the truth was I was too consumed with hate to really pay him any mind, thinking of other men to fuck that were close to Cyclone to get back at him. It was barely a minute after I enacted my plan that his bitch came out with guns blazing wanting to get rid of everybody in his camp. The thing that got everybody was that Cyclone went about it like a little punk and let it happen without even bothering to open his mouth. He might not have looked out for everybody that helped him become a household name, but he went out of his way to make sure that I was good before he jumped the broom. He gave me enough money to put down a sizeable payment on a decent two-bedroom home with plenty left over to wild out and sustain me for spell.

# # # # #

The second I bounced my motorcycle into my driveway behind my car it felt as if I had dumped the weight of the world off my shoulders. I was fresh from the post office that bright and sunny afternoon after sending Cyclone and his new bride their belated wedding gift. I knew that I didn't have to do that shit, but it was my way of accepting that he made his choice to let go and I was free to do the same.

I barely got off of my new wheels with this incredible feeling when I saw my putty brown-skinned neighbor from across the street shuffle his way over in his socks and flip flops. Sam didn't even have to open his mouth for me not to know that while I had learned to let go, another piece of baggage in my life hadn't.

"Big Man stopped by again," Sam announced in that sexy Tone Loc-deep voice of his sporting a crisp low cut fade and a trimmed long beard that hung off of his short fat face by a couple of inches. "I think he ran over to the convenient store. He'll probably be back in a few minutes."

I let out a long groan, and slowly got back on my bike to walk it behind Sam over to his place. He smoothly ducked through the iron front door to be on further lookout for me while I continued on the side of the house through the wooden gate leading to the backyard.

Antonio had been a thorn in my side ever since he decided not to head back east for his new job. He decided that our "love" was too powerful just to be ignored. He had to stick around to see where something so real could lead. I was trying to be nice. I tried sending the boy off on a good foot, but I just had to be frank with him. The dick was amazing, but it was never going to work out. He knew of at least thirty guys that had fucked me since the first night we met. Even my liberated ass knew that it was only a matter of time when the thought of all those men plugging my holes was going to fuck with his mind, and I was doomed to be on the receiving end of it. I'm not in the business of dealing with that shit anymore. He called himself addressing my concerns by telling me that he didn't care about my past. He said that if I hadn't gotten other dudes out of my system that he was cool if I still messed around as long as he could watch. He was down with that, too. He thought I should've jumped on that bandwagon because he moved into the extended stay near the expressway waiting for me to change my mind. It is only when he was between assignments that he stood outside of my door telling me he was nothing without "our love."

I came back there with my bike not intending to find Tory back there tending to his cannabis patch hidden amongst the tall plants in his yard. I didn't mean to startle him. I thought he clearly heard me come on back since it wasn't as if it was hard to miss me on his small space of earth back there. But apparently he did, and I spooked him, looking back at me like a mischievous child that just got caught with his hand in the forbidden cookie jar.

"Oh, it's just you," Tory said breathing a sigh of relief, his thick rusty brown hair sticking out with sweat under his weathered baseball cap. "I thought you were somebody else."

Tory paused, looked at me with my bike in tow and mutual aggravation in his face. He jerked his head over to the small tool shed behind him.

Crenshaw wasn't where I wanted to be, but it wasn't nearly as bad as a place as I had originally made it out to be either. My neighbors overall were pretty cool. They did a fantastic job of looking out for me, just like they did back east. The major difference being that I couldn't do as great of a job keeping my business under wraps like I used to. Not with a large black man pacing frantically in front of my door begging for me to give "us" a chance.

I tried telling myself that I was just being paranoid about the whole situation. He wasn't so loud that everybody could hear him. Telling myself that people living around me were too busy paying attention to what was going on at their house to really pay that much attention to mine. If I had to be really honest about it though, I would say most people only speculated what was going on. But since Antonio and I did get off into that switching stuff, and still walked around proudly packing our dicks, I don't think anybody truly thought there was more to our picture. Though, there were times when I felt like I was cold busted. In particular, by some of the mature ex-cons that would sometimes ride by my house and blow me a gangster's kiss. If it wasn't for me already dealing with one crazy black man too many, I might've been crazy enough to go there, especially with that off-looking dark-skinned dude with those crazy blue eyes.

"I take it that Fat Boy wants his good kush back again, huh?" Tory added as I tried to make my way into the house through the backdoor.

"Please, not now, man," I pleaded, praying that Sam might have one of his infamous protein shakes ready for me to sample. "I was having a kick-ass day before I heard about that son of a bitch coming around."

"I told you about giving away my best shit like that. You got dudes banging on your door wanting extra helpings. I don't see why you don't make life easy on yourself and just throw a dude a pack of Oreos into traffic and be done with. And just let me have a little bit of some of that he's craving." Tory licked his lips and slightly chuckled, though the look in his eyes suggested that he was as serious as a heart attack.

I just looked back at him while he puckered his lips ready to blow me a kiss before I ducked inside.

# # # # #

"I got your bed ready." Tory announced balancing his solid frame on his huge foot as he leaned over to smooth out the sheets he spread on top of the sofa.

Night had fallen on the West Coast, and obviously I was still there at his house. Antonio was visible from across the street sitting in front of my doorstep drinking one of those big cheap bottles of beer, looking like he was a sip short of stretching out over my short sidewalk waiting on my return.

I had just stepped out of the kitchen into the living room sipping on my red cup with a tinge of lustful regret itching in my pants. I had just spent the better part of the night turning Tory down on his invitation to join him in his bed for the hundredth time, and there he goes looking damn good in nothing else but those white and blue-green striped boxers.

It wasn't so much him as it was the wild hairs on his thick hairy legs that looked as if they could be quite ticklish next to my sensitive flesh.

If Antonio was a stalker, Tory was just simply annoying.

Tory was the sole owner of the pale orangey house that he shared with his cousin Sam. He previously spent that last nineteen years of his career working for one of the major utility companies before getting injured and having to file for workman's comp and later for disability. He was injured, but he wasn't disabled. He just didn't want to give his life back over to The Man anymore. He came over to my house shortly after I got settled in trying to sell me some of his homegrown weed. He took one look at me, found out that I was single and wasted no time making a play for me. He just couldn't believe that a sweet Southern boy like me chose to live all by myself in this big Southern California house with nobody at night to cover me from the rampant gang violence. When I didn't take him up on his offer (already knowing that Crenshaw never was notorious for gang activity), he promised to look out for me. He didn't want me to get eaten by the wolves out there. He didn't leave without offering up his other services to help me around the house since he was also a talented handyman. I begrudgingly needed him sooner rather than later to help me stop a sprouting leak and a few other things, like pulling a gun out for my protection and providing a safe hideout spot when the police didn't bother to show up nearly as quickly as I would've liked.

There was some sexual tension there. I won't lie. Nothing is hotter than two sexually-charged masculine men fighting it. But even if the circumstances didn't lend themselves itself to the situation at play, I still wouldn't bother to give him the time of day. Tory was such an arrogant ass most of the time. And not the kind that usually later proved to be sexy as hell after he's got under your skin either. He already thought I owed him for being a good neighbor. It would be all over if he was just halfway decent in bed. I would never hear the end of it. He would be worse than my other problem sitting over there. Though, it might be worth it to know that there was somebody nearby to scratch an itch when I didn't feel like reaching for it. No. I can't even think like that about him. He already had an ego problem. His biggest problem was that he thought he was God's gift to the world because of his high yellow skin tone as if it was the sum total of his very existence. Because of it, he thought he could say and do just about anything to anybody and get away with it.

Tory was an arrogant son of a bitch, but he wasn't an ugly one to my dismay. He was cute in an easily overlooked sort of way. He probably could've shine a lot more if he just fell back a little and got over himself. He probably could've score an extra few point if he freely nodded that his cousin was actually the better looking of the two, and it had nothing to do with him being significantly younger. Sam had that Big Daddy thing working for him at twenty-eight that most men never get a chance to master anywhere in their late maturity. Tory had to have been scraping forty or just pasted it but looked a decade younger than his age and actually acted another decade younger than he looked.

"Good night," Tory said, heading off down the hall to his bedroom.

"Good night." I said, thinking that his beefy body was really sweet covered in a thin layer of hair.

# # # # #

It had to be about three o'clock that morning when I woke up again for the fourth time that night. I was just horny like the other times before, sleepily teasing both my dick and the outer lips of my puckered hole waiting for this wave of lust to pass. I thought if I held out for morning, when Antonio had cleared, I could get in front of my computer and pull up one of my favorite X-rated clips. I could've also done what I needed to do and roll over but felt that the scent might be telling on me later on. And then it hit me. I had no reason to be playing with myself. I had two men that were willing to hook me up if I just asked. If I went back across the street, I knew what I would be getting. The problem with that is that I knew exactly what I would be getting, which was the very reason I was over here. Behind Door Number Two wasn't much better. But behind it lingered a mystery though. I heard a lot of mouth over the past few months but wasn't sure if it could be backed by anything. So I thought about it long and deep. If I let him get at me, I would never hear the end of it. If he was half as good as he preached, then I might not be so resistant to give him his props. If he sucked, he could never say that I never game him a shot and be free to critique his flawed skills.

Tory was snoring soundly when I cracked the door to his bedroom. I quickly got a whiff of some weed still lingering about. Even in his sleep, he was an arrogant jackass. Sleeping on his back in the center of the bed with his head tilted back into the pillows and arms stretched out as if he was a king in the middle of some imaginary threesome. I kept asking myself did I really want to go through with this, as I thought about retreating and ducking into the second bedroom. It was worth a crack. The only thing that stopped me was that I actually believed Sam when he said that he was straight. And besides, it didn't help much that his older cousin liked me and was claiming me as his personal property.

So I pulled back the covers and slowly climbed in next to him. I still wasn't sure if I wanted to wake him up just yet. Just in case I suddenly had a change of heart. All the while I was in his bed I kept on questioning what I was going to do next. It was like I was a virgin all over again, not knowing what moves to make. At first, I thought about just waking him up. Let him know that I was in his bed if he was still game. I had to stop right there. I had to remind myself that I had better skills than that. I needed to be a little bit more seductive. Considering that he had been working hard to get to this place. Then I thought about waking him up by running my fingers through the dusting of hair on his chest and down its skipping trail that ended somewhere below his waistline where his warm banana resided.

But in trying to make up my mind of what to do next, I put my head on one of his many pillows underneath his arm. The closeness of our bodies strangely took me back to those nights alone with Cyclone. I was always under him holding him tight while we dreamt. It was usually about that time of the morning when he would slip away from my grip and climb under the sheets. I don't know what position I started out in, but I would always be flat on my back when he took his big hands and parted my cheeks just enough to fit his face and tongue in all the right places. I woke up plenty of mornings moaning pure ecstasy into. He tried convincing me that it was all about me, but we both knew that it was really all about him, about me not saying no to him when the time came when he needed to put that hefty dick somewhere.

I wasn't even aware of all that I was doing until I had my nose in the slit of his boxers, taking in the clean musty scent of his wiry pubes. I kissed the sluggish shaft and licked the length of it nice and slow before nursing the hooded beast in my warm wet mouth. Tory was quick to respond with a commanding erection that grew leaps and bounds, like an old car antenna out of its rear, but the man himself was slow to stir, not sure what was going on.

"You got that for me, don't you?" He mumbled. He did it in such a way with the slits of his eyes barely open that led me to believe that he thought he was still in a dream-like state that this wasn't quite real. Not yet.

I could've done a few things to change that line of thinking. Instead, I decided to be the good freak that I was and play along with it as he rushed to close his eyelids again. I insured that my touch was dreamlike. The way I held it, the way I stroked it. Wet thirsty gulps of a good blowjob that should've been present were replaced by the torturous tongue lashes using the flat side of tongue.

"Oh, damn, baby," he moaned, putting his hands behind his head with my lips sliding along his velvety smooth mass. If this really was a dream for him, he had no interest in walking up from it anytime soon.

Tory had an awkward dick. It was chunky and uneven and was downright ugly in a cute sort of way. His balls were odd, though. His sac was small and sweet, but they were packed with a pair that made them look larger than they were but by typical standard weren't measuring up to par, licking them slowly just the same.

"That is my nutts," he gurgled with pleasure, with the slits of his eyes lazily parting open.

I saw his hand move slowly to the top of my head. It was as if he was trying to fight moving it. As if he dared reached out and touch me that his dream would come to an abrupt end. He scared himself more than he scared me when his hand landed on the top of my head, and he still felt the same incredible sensation.

"I knew you couldn't resist me. I knew it. I just knew it. I felt it in my bones," he said wearily, swinging his other hand out to the side of my face to make sure I was real.

His hand was steady on top of my head bouncing in his lap as my mouth got hungrier for him. He rode this feeling for a while, telling me that it was driving him crazy just knowing that I was in the next room lying on that crappy sofa instead of his bed.

"Enough of that," he smiled. "Come up here. I want to take care of you like I suppose to."

I snaked my way up to him. I was expecting a few kisses across my face and neck, but nothing prepared me for the kisses he put across my lips. It was like his tongue was hungry for his taste, and he was going to explore every inch of my mouth to get it. If I wasn't hard before my dick was certainly on brick then. I was so caught up that I didn't get to see how smooth he was with his game. All the while he was kissing me and making me feel this certain way, he had slipped on a condom and was lubing up me at the same time.

It was like I had no say so in the matter, but just fine with it just the same. Tory had me on my back so fast that if it wasn't for his hands behind my knees I would have never known that my feet was already braced against his shoulders. He had me so open and so pre-greased that it felt like he was boning a cloud in me. He worked my booty, pinning my arms against the pillows to gain better access. I thought he was doing this to get better control, just to go for his. But that couldn't be further from the truth. It was like he knew where to go with me and what to do to make me hot, to appeal to intimate freak in me. He was stroking like we had been doing this for a long time and every place he hit was just the right place.

"Bounce that ass, boy. Bounce that ass." He demanded. I had no idea that the bastard had worked me into such a heated sweat. I thought I was just lying back and enjoying the ride when I felt the full force of my feet press against his chest, and I was grinding my hips hard against him, wanting and begging for one more pump. "Tell me how got that shit is, my dude."

"Damn, dawg, it's good. It's good." I said, vomiting up my old street lingo

"It's the best? Huh?"

"It's the best. Damn, Daddy, it's the fucking best! No lie." He had me crying.

"That's what I like to hear." He said with the arrogance creeping back up in his voice. As good as he had me feeling, I didn't mind letting him have that one.

I had made up my mind that I was going to let him have a few more after he grabbed the ball and started taking these long deep jabs that made me appreciate that this wasn't just dick in ass. This was him and me. And when I got the sense of that, he went back to fucking me, and I felt his dick tense up. He didn't need to say anything. He just looked at me in my daze and just poured everything he had into the condom inside of me.

I don't remember much after that. I don't remember even rubbing one out to go to sleep. I just remember waking up spent to these pair of eyes staring back at me skinning and grinning like he was certain he was about to get some more. Damn that arrogant ass.

YELLOW AND WHITE
By: Sam Mason

This is Sam Mason's first published story.

Greg is a veterinarian. He stares out of the window into the dreary afternoon. It has been raining nonstop all morning, and still people keep coming in with their sick pets. It wouldn't be a problem if the vet wasn't understaffed today because they called in "sick," but Greg knows the truth; they didn't want to come into work in bad weather. They'd rather stay home where it is dry and away from dogs that have exploding diarrhea. He wishes he could go home, but duty calls and he must cure the puppies of diarrhea and cats of stomach viruses.

As the day wares on and one of the cats he is treating finally manages to throw up on his shoes, he is ready to call it quits and go home. He is already behind schedule because a poor dog had a bad reaction to the shot he gave it, and he had to wait for another vet to deliver the medicine for the sick dog. Greg decides that he will leave after an hour. It is almost closing time anyway, so leaving an hour early wouldn't hurt anybody or any animal. He will deal with them tomorrow.

That is when Matt, a regular, comes in shaking rain water off his bright yellow umbrella. His golden retriever is beside him trying to play with the umbrella. Matt is an hour late, but Greg quickly excuses him because of the awful weather; it must being making traffic a nightmare. Out of all the regulars that Greg sees, he likes Matt the most. He's just a charming and friendly person with an energetic personality that is contagious, and Greg couldn't help but to smile as soon as he sees Matt.

"Happy is finally here to get his shots updated," Matt said in a voice that is rich and thick like honey while smiling so brightly that it is blinding. Greg goes over to Happy and gives him a pat on the head while looking at Matt.

Every time Greg sees him, he is always wearing yellow. Right now he is wearing a yellow windbreaker with white slacks and yellow tennis shoes. Matt's sky blue eyes are shiny with happiness and his long blond hair is out flowing over his shoulders and down his back. Greg's hands inch to feel the softness of his hair.

"I understand why you would be late because of the rain and all. I'm just glad you both arrived here safe," Greg says as he leads Matt and Happy into the lab room to get his shots updated. Once Greg has updated Happy's shots, he is delighted when Matt decides to stay after to talk with him.

"Well now Happy's shots are updated," Greg says as he stares at the dog's charts. Matt is pleased with the good news and shakes Greg's hand.

"That's good and before I go, Greg. Can I ask you something?"

"Sure, you can ask me anything, Matt," he tells him,

"I noticed that the pen you are using has a gym logo on. I am looking for a gym that has an indoor track in it because I am training to run in a marathon to raise awareness about animal cruelty and also to raise money for animal shelters," Matt says and Greg looks at the pen in his hand before handing it to Matt.

"I go to this gym and it is a great gym with a very good indoor track. You should join and we can be workout partners. The number is also on the pen," he tells him.

"That would be cool, and you can run in the marathon with me," Matt says while giving him a wink that makes Greg's heart skip a beat.

"Yeah, I would like that. I'll do anything to help protect animals," he says and leaves unsaid: *I'll do anything just to be near you.*

"You don't know how much this means to me that you want to do this. Just think of all the animals you'll be saving just by running. I don't know how to repay you," he says, and Greg thinks of many ways he could repay him and shakes his head to erase the naughty thoughts as he smiles up at Matt who is taller than he by a foot.

"You don't have to repay me; like I said, I'll do anything to help protect animals. It's part of my job," he says and Matt nods his head in agreement.

"It's still a good thing what you are doing. I guess I better get going. See ya later," Matt says waving at him with the pen in his hand as he walks out of the office with his dog.

Greg leans against the receptionist desk because his legs feel like jelly as he watches all that beautiful yellow disappear from sight. He never had an experience with anybody before where their mere presence makes him weak in the knees.

He can't help feeling giddy as he gets ready to leave and as he leaves he notices that the rain has stopped and a rainbow is high in the sky. *Matt made the rain stop and caused the rainbow to appear*, Greg thinks while smiling to himself as he gets into his car and drives off with the thoughts of Matt working out with him all sweaty dressed in yellow.

When he gets home, he gets a text from Matt telling him that he has just joined the gym and wanting to know if they could work together tomorrow. Greg texts him back saying sure he would like that and he will see him there. All the while he is grinning like a damn fool.

The next day, Greg doesn't see Matt anywhere in the gym to his disappointment. So, he decides to do some incline bench presses to pass time until Matt shows up. He is doing fine on his back lifting the weight up above him. His mind is on controlling his breathing and lifting the weight. He is fine until a pair of yellow shorts hover above his head. His eyes go right toward the large bulge in the center as his mouth starts to water and his arms shakes as he loses focus.

"Careful, Greg or you'll drop the weight and hurt yourself," Matt says reaching to help Greg keep the weight steady. Needing time to recover, Greg puts the weight up before he sits up.

"Hey, Matt, I didn't see you around earlier, did you just get here?" he asks a little out of breath as he watches Matt nod his head.

"Yeah, I just changed into my gym gear and was going to go run on the track when I saw you. So, I came over to see if you needed a spotter." Matt says and Greg looks at him, he is wearing yellow shorts and a white tank top, with yellow running shoes and this time his fabulous long blond hair is pulled back into a ponytail.

He had always been attracted to Matt since he first met him and his dog Happy at the vet a year ago. The attractiveness only increased when he discovered that they both have a fondness for animals. Matt just so happens to be an animal's rights activist, which just piled on the sexiness for Greg. Matt has it all; the looks, brains, and the heart. What more can a guy ask for?

"Umm, I was going to stop and take a little break before doing something else," Greg says.

"Okay, that's cool. When you are finished working out, what are your plans for tonight." Matt asks, and Greg wonders if he is leading to asking him out, when he remembers that he does have plans tonight.

"It's my friend's birthday and she invited me to come to her party," Greg says a little disappointed because he rather be with him.

"That's cool. We more than likely don't have the same friends but wish her a happy birthday for me anyway," Matt says.

"Okay, I will," Greg says with a pause.

"Well I'm going to go run around the track for a bit, let me know when you are rested up and want to work out together," Matt says.

"I'm rested enough. I'll go run with you," Greg says and together they walk to the track before doing some stretches. As they start to run, they talk about their jobs and the animals they save and the crazy people that hurt animals. Greg feels their bond tightening and by the time they finish their run and ready to go home, Greg is madly in love with Matt.

At the birthday party, Greg is going out of his mind with boredom, all there is to do is mingle with the world dullest group of people he has ever had the misfortune to know. There isn't even any music playing, and his friend calls this a birthday party. All he can think about is Matt. It gets to a point where he starts to think that he is seeing Matt everywhere at the party.

"I guess I was wrong; we do have the same friend." Greg's body reacts before his mind does when he hears the honey rich voice as he turns around to see Matt dressed in a yellow T-shirt and pale blue jeans.

"Why didn't you tell me that you were going to a birthday party as well? We would have figured it out sooner that we were going to the same party and could have come here together," Greg says.

"I was a last minute invite. So how do you know the birthday girl, Jessica?" Matt asks.

"Though her dog, I'm her veterinarian and Mrs. Peaches loves me. How about you? How do you know Jessica?" Greg asks as they both look at the birthday girl mingling with the other guests.

"Our dogs are more than just friends, they are a couple," Matt says.

"Maybe that's why you got invited at the last minute," Greg says and they both start to laugh as Matt moves closer to Greg still smiling.

"Yeah, Jessica doesn't like my dog and whenever we are at the dog park she rushes Peaches around, so she won't get close to Happy."

"Now what kind of person would hate a dog named Happy?"

"Jessica," there is a pause as Matt leans into Greg's ear. He gets a whiff of Matt's sweet smelling cologne and is taken away to paradise.

"How about we get out of here and go have a party of our own. I know this comedy club not far from here that is open all the time. They also serve the best veggie burgers in the world. We can go and have a few laughs over a couple of veggie burgers and drinks," Matt says his breath tickling Greg's ear making him shiver in delight.

"That sounds good, and I love veggie burgers, but I can't party too hard I have to work in the morning," Greg says.

"Yeah, I got work, too, come on," Matt says leading the way out of the party and Greg follows him down two blocks where the comedy club is. Matt pays for their tickets and they go in and order a couple of veggie burgers and a couple of beers. Once Greg bites into one of the burgers, he has to agree with Matt that this is the best veggie burger he has ever tasted.

The comedy club is mostly for amateurs. Anybody who thinks they are funny gets fifteen minutes to prove how funny they are. Tonight they are lucky, the amateurs are actually funny and before they know it, they are laughing the night away. Greg loves the way Matt laughs so carefree and young.

He feels like a moth to flame around Matt, and he wants Matt to burn him up with the fire of passion. As they sit next to each listening and laughing at the comedians, Matt looks at him and their eyes lock; his sky blues against Greg's earth tone brown eyes. He never wants this night to end and he gets the feeling that Matt doesn't want this night to end either.

But all good things must come to end and to Greg's added delight, Matt walks him back to Jessica's house where his car is parked.

"Can I give you a ride home?" he asks Matt who shakes his head while jerking a thumb behind him up the street.

"No, need but thanks anyway, I live four blocks from here. I'll see you at the gym," Matt says and leans forward towards him and Greg's breathe catches in his throat. Is he going to kiss him? Greg wonders and he wants him to do it so badly, to feel Matt's lips against his own lips.

Instead Matt gives him a hug and walks away waving goodbye to him as he leaves. Even though he is clearly disappointed and let down about not kissing Matt, when Greg goes home to bed, he is smiling and still thinking about Matt while having biggest boner he has ever had in his whole life.

On Saturday afternoon in the gym, Greg watches from the water cooler as Matt runs laps around the indoor track. It is hard not to notice Matt in his bright yellow T-shirt that is so tight you can see his heart beating. And a pair of yellow shorts so short that Greg could tell that he is packing heat and hung like a horse.

The yellow only enhances Matt's golden tan skin, long wavy blond hair in a ponytail, and the sky blue of his eyes. Greg's dick hardens, and for a second he thinks he is going to bust a nut as he continues to stare at Matt as he sprints around the track. The yellow shorts showing off his nice long legs as the muscles in his legs flexes as they propel him forward, Greg even likes how the shorts hug his round ass.

To Greg, he is eye catching on his own, the yellow just intensifies it. Greg makes up his mind that today he is going to stop playing around and finally ask Matt out on a date. When Matt is done with his run, he jogs over to Greg and pours himself some water from the water cooler and takes a drink. All thoughts escape Greg's mind as he inhales the smells of sweat and cologne on Matt. It is like smelling a sweaty cantaloupe taking Greg far away into dreamland.

"Hey, Greg, I believe we will be ready for the marathon in no time now. I enjoy working out here." Matt says bringing Greg back to reality, and even though he is a little out of breath from running, his voice is still thick like honey. He leans against the wall beside the water cooler. Greg shrugs his shoulders.

"I'm glad you like it and you are certainly fit to run any marathon," he says while looking him up and down and when he realizes what he is doing, he quickly changes the subject hoping that Matt doesn't get the wrong idea.

"So how is your dog, Happy? He wasn't so happy when I gave him the shots," Greg says, and they share a laugh.

"Happy is good and playful as always," Matt says before leaning forward toward, Greg giving him a wink,

"Want to know what else I've enjoyed?" Matt asks and Greg leans forward with him,

"Sure, tell me what else you enjoy?" Greg asks him while smiling as his heart starts to race. *How is it that Matt has no idea of the effect he has on him?*

"I enjoy you watching me as I run around the track. That is one of the reasons why I wanted to join this gym, to be closer to you. I really like you, Greg."

"What can I say? Yellow is very eye catching and so are you, Matt," he says before his emotions take over. "Why did you wait to now to tell me that you like me? I really like you, too, Matt. I … I just wasn't sure that you felt the same way. Then at the comedy club, I got the feeling that maybe you did like me, but then you walked away and I…" Matt places his index finger against his lips shutting him up,

"I walked away that night because I wanted to kiss you, but I didn't want to be forceful or seem too needy. I didn't want to scare you and ruin our friendship, so I left."

"Matt, I feel the same way, and today, I was trying to build up enough courage to ask you out on a date," Greg says while feeling his face getting hot as he watches Matt staring at him looking thoughtful, "Are you still building up your courage to ask me out?"

"Do you want to go out for dinner and maybe go dancing with me after we finish working out?" he says embarrassed as his face is now blood red, he looks away. Matt grabs his chin and lifts his head up, so he could look into Greg's eyes.

"I would love to go out with you, Greg. You are a really special guy."

"I think you are special, too, Matt. I can't get you out of my mind and because of you, yellow is now officially my favorite color," he says and Matt starts to laugh,

"Well, yellow has always been my favorite color, if you haven't figured that out by now," he says before pulling Greg closer to him then lowers his head to kiss him on the lips. Greg's heart is pounding in his chest as everything around them seems to melt away into that kiss.

He wraps his arms around Matt's waist as he feverishly kisses Matt back. He welcomes Matt's tongue in his mouth greeting it with his own tongue. Matt pulls away from him breathing hard and Greg follows him like a sick puppy. Matt gives him a nut busting wink and smile. "I am done with my workout and I am going to hit the showers. You should join if you are not ...yellow," Matt says before finishing his water and jogs away to the locker room. Greg finishes his water as well before he follows after all that sexy yellow.

Greg finds Matt alone in the locker room pulling down his shorts, revealing a pair of yellow bikini briefs, Greg stares mesmerized as Matt peels the T-shirt and briefs off.

"It's just the two of us now, Greg," Matt says standing before him in all his glory; smooth tan skin, nice firm muscles, abs as hard as bricks, and a dick so long and thick it looks like a three-D animation. Greg goes to him like a thirsty man to a watering hole.

Their lips lock in a heated embrace, tongues caressing each other as spit is being exchanged. Matt pushes him up against a locker pinning him with his body, and Greg can feel the pulsating need of Matt's dick pressing against his leg. If this is a dream, Greg never wants to wake up from it.

Matt starts to kiss and bite the side of his neck causing him to moan and arch his head back in ecstasy. His hands go into Matt's hair freeing it of its ponytail. While his hands are busy in his hair, Matt is sucking and licking on his neck.

He couldn't take it anymore. Greg kisses, licks, sucks, and bites his way down Matt's body, he licks away all the sweat, enjoying the saltiness and overall taste of him. His mouth beelines for the massive meat between Matt's legs, his tongue rapidly licking the bulbous head tasting the salty precum as it leaks out. His skin is so tantalizing, he is like a drug to Greg.

Without wasting any more time Greg devours Matt's dick taking it all the way to the back of his throat. His eyes tears up, but he holds the position, swallowing hard. The fine hairs on Matt's balls tickling his chin. He slowly pulls back some before going back down, enjoying the feel of Matt's dick expanding in his mouth.

He sticks his index finger into Matt's tight hole and is awarded by Matt moaning low in his throat as he thrusts himself deeper into his mouth almost choking him as a spurt of precum went down his throat. His mouth and finger works as a unit, one going up and down while the other is going in and out in a rapid pace to get Matt off.

"Greg, I'm coming bro," Matt moans seconds before a big burst of cum fills Greg's mouth, which is followed by waves and waves of more cum. Greg happily swallows it all before getting up and giving Matt another kiss on the lips.

"How about we go get cleaned up?" he says while taking off his own clothes, his dick is thick and pulsating against his leg. Matt follows him into a shower stall and under the hot steamy water they leather each other up with soap.

Greg loves the feel of Matt's tone muscles covered in soap. His dick is aching with need so Greg takes his soapy dick and shoves it into Matt's hot tight ass. He never would have thought in a million years that he would be able to do something like this with Matt.

The feel of his tight opening rubbing against his dick is almost overwhelming. He is on the verge of coming right then and there. It takes all of Greg's self-control to not come early. He wants to savor this moment. It is getting more difficult because Matt starts to back up into him as he goes in while making sounds that are so enticing. He wishes he could stay like this forever, inside of Matt.

This is payment for all of the time they spent together as the veterinarian taking care of the owner's dog. This is a year of pent up sexual frustration driving in and out of Matt's ass.

Matt puts his hands on the shower wall for support as Greg pounds his ass with no mercy. Matt's moaning in pleasure only fuels Greg on and before he comes; he pulls out of Matt's ass to come on his back. As Greg watches his hot white cum pooling onto Matt's skin, he notices that white is a sexy color on Matt just like yellow.

ONE OF THE BOYS?
By Don Mika

Don Mika started writing at an early age and has been published in numerous anthologies. He can be reached for comments at Little-big-mann@yahoo.com.

My senior year of high school was hell. Being an army brat, I was on my third school by the second semester. I had learned not to make friends because that would only make moving away harder. My appearance made this decision an easy accomplishment. My hair had grown down below my shoulders, and I often hid my face behind it – and also behind heavy layers of black mascara and lipstick. The toll of moving and trying to find myself in a sea of cruel adolescents had caused a dramatic weight loss, and my clothes seemed to swallow me whole.

Even though the baggy look was popular among my hip-hop influenced peers, it made me even more of social outcast because my previous wardrobe had been devised of punk and gothic garments. I looked more like a little girl playing in her father's closet than I exuded the badass image that I hoped.

Even though I am Native-American and Puerto Rican, people referred to me as 9-11, because they assumed I was Arabic and therefore solely responsible for the fall of the towers. I was the victim of constant verbal and physical abuse, which I usually shrugged off. Being the effeminate guy at a previous military school had taught me to develop a thick layer of skin, just as being multiracial in an all-white school had taught me before.

Usually, the physical abuse was limited to spit balls in my hair or boogers being wiped on the back of my shirt. I only truly feared for my safety in gym class because Alpha males, who constantly joked that I looked like a girl and threatened to rape me in the showers, surrounded me. I opted not to participate in gym, fearing breaking a sweat and having to take a shower. I spent the time watching other guys de-shirt and run up and down the court, their skin glistening, a bright blur of flesh toned rainbow streaks. I had begun to see everything in streaks since I had discovered the joys of cocaine and marijuana, the two friends that were sure to be waiting for me no matter what unheard of town my dad decided to drag us to next.

One day I sat in gym class, deep in a daydream about Blake Webb, a six-foot tall black guy, who was sometimes nice to me, because we had math class together and because I would let him copy my papers. I looked down, noticing the biggest erection I had ever achieved and busied myself trying to hide it with my oversized sweatshirt. I was so engulfed in the fantasy that I hadn't even heard the whistle blow, signaling shower time. I felt three sets of hands grab me. A backpack was pulled over my head, and I was dragged into the locker room, wondering why the coach, who was five feet away, did nothing to aid me.

"Strip, bitch!" I was demanded, and before I could comply or resist, I was punched in the head. I fell to the floor wriggling in pain. I reached to remove the bag from my head but was kicked in the temple and told to leave it there, so I did. I didn't know exactly how many guys were there, but from the impact of that first blow, I was sure that it wouldn't have mattered if it were two or twenty. I never was much of a fighter.

"Why are yawl doing this to me?" I asked, as I felt my clothes being ripped from my body. Two sets of hands grabbed my shoulders, and two more fastened around each of my legs. I was hoisted up on one of the musty benches, and warned to not move or reach for the bag again. I obeyed and trembled inside at the feel of someone sliding his penis up and down the slit of my ass.

"Look at all this ass he got under them clothes!" my humper exclaimed. "I told yawl this faggot ass bitch should be a girl. And then he got the nerve to paint his fingernails black."

"I just like being different," I tried to explain, but I was punched in the side and told to not speak again.

"We ought to fuck this bitch!" someone at the back of the crowd suggested and then hocked a ball of mucus unto my bare skin.

"Fuck that! Enough of that faggot shit!" I heard a voice protest, and the guy who was humping me was pushed away. I heard footsteps surrounding me from all angels and fought against my impulse to rip the bag away and see the faces of my many potential rapists or murders.

"Don't be scared, 9-11!" a deep, almost familiar voice declared. "We aren't going to kill you, not yet anyway."

"I've never hurt anybody!" I spat out, disrupting my inner chant of the twenty-third psalm. I truly was scared for my life.

"We ain't going to hurt you either!" someone laughed. "We just making sure you shower today. We don't know what you do in Ireland, but…"

"Iran," someone else thought they had corrected.

"What the fuck ever! We take showers here, homeboy. You been in this class for fourteen days and that mean we owe you fourteen showers. I'm going to give you the first one."

I shuttered in discuss at the feel of his urine saturating my hair through the already stale smelling backpack. I cried out in pain as piss and leather belts pelted my skin. One by one and two by two, they all joined in, until so much urine was aimed at my face that I couldn't breathe. I prayed harder, hoping that my eighteen-year run as a recluse wasn't going to end by me being drowned in jock urine.

Even when the last of the pissers had filed away I felt more and more urine. I thought that one of the guys must have an elephant's bladder until I heard the familiar pump of a high-powered water gun. There was a steady stream of who knows how many days old piss covering my head, making the bag cling to my head, and even filling my mouth and nose.

"Chill man; that's enough!" somebody insisted as I vomited violently.

The stream ceased, but their laughter seemed infinite. The puke mixed with the urine, and caused the bag to cling to my face even more. I was certain by now that I would suffocate.

When it was long over, and they all had piled into the shower, I still lay there, my face covered by the puke-filled piss bag. I would have rather died at that moment than let them see me cry, even though I was sure they could hear me anyway. I didn't remove the bag, not even after I heard them file out of the locker room, spitting on me, or getting in one final kick or punch as they left.

"Get up, man," I heard a gentle voice say to me, and I lay there, ignoring it, until the bag was pulled from my face. I opened my eyes, which sill stung from piss, and saw that is was Blake. Apparently, he had gym the period after I did.

"Just leave me alone!" I protested as he tried to help me up, but he ignored me and I was pulled to my feet, and then towards the shower. On instinct, I began to fight, but was seized by his strong arms so that I couldn't move.

"I'm trying to help you. You know I wouldn't hurt you; stop swinging at me!"

I crouched down under the shower stream, so hysterical that I vomited again. Blake began to lather my hair and face up with his body wash. I heard footsteps and felt a second pair of hands aiding in my bath. I opened my eyes to find that we had been joined by his best friend, Malcolm.

"Who did this shit to you?" Blake wanted to know. Unfortunately, I had the same question.

"We have to teach this kid to defend himself," Malcolm observed, helping me to my feet.

I looked down, and Blake and Malcolm were both fully erect. I instantly sprung to attention myself. Blake's penis was even larger than I had dreamed, a coal-black ten inches bouncing between his muscular thighs. Malcolm was only an inch or so behind him, but his penis was thicker, and it was so hard that it jumped up and down even when he was completely still. His yellowish-brown skin was stretched so far that it was turning a bright pink.

"I told you, Blake," Malcolm smiled, and their method of washing me grew more sensual. His hands began to creep over my private places. I thought I would pass out from the excitement, but I was too nervous that we would get caught to enjoy it.

"You are coming with us for lunch break!" Blake insisted. The water was turned off and we all exited, toweling off with the same damp towel.

My clothes were ripped beyond repair, so I was given a dirty pair of Malcolm's shorts, which were too short, yet fell off my waist and had to be held up with my shoestrings. Blake let me use a T-shirt, which fit me like a dress, so the shorts became obsolete.

"Where are we going?" I asked as we piled into Malcolm's pick-up truck.

"Don't worry about it," Blake whispered, caressing my thigh. "From today on out, nobody will bother you again. Me and Malcolm got your back. Believe me?"

"I want to."

"You got a girlfriend?" Malcolm wanted to know.

"I don't have any friends."

"You have two now," Blake promised as we backed into the driveway of an enormous house.

"This is my uncle's spot," Malcolm ensured me. "It's cool. I'm watching it for him while he's on vacation. That means we got the place all to ourselves."

"Why didn't you fight back?" Blake questioned once we were inside the huge house.

"Because I like living."

"Hit me!" Malcolm demanded stepping in front of me. "Go on; pretend I'm one of the guys from the gym and I'm grabbing on your ass, and trying to pull you into the shower. What are you going to do?"

Blake sat back on the couch, opening a hot can of soda as he awaited the show.

"I'm not hitting you!"

"'Cause you a pussy, 9-11!" he literally spat at me and shoved me so hard that I toddled back, almost tripping over the glass table. "I'd piss on you, too, if it wasn't a waste of good water!"

"Why you doing this?" I cried. "What was all this shit about you guys wanting to protect me? You bring me here just to beat me some more?"

"Nobody can do shit to you that you don't let them do, 9-11!" Malcolm laughed, and slapped me playfully. "So, what you going to do? You going to be my bitch, or you going to fight me?"

"Fuck you!" I screamed heading for the door, but Blake leapt before me like an angry cougar, blocking my way.

"This is why they keep fucking with you at school! You can't run away from everything all the time; and no matter how you ignore some things, they don't go away. Malcolm wasn't really going to hurt you, but he just wanted to make you fight back."

"I can't!" I screamed, releasing the furry I had bottled all day. "I shouldn't have to!"

82

"We shouldn't have had to wash somebody else's piss off of your face either, but we don't live in a perfect world," Malcolm added, cradling me in his arms as I slumped to the floor with tears. "Don't cry! Stop that right now, or I will really fuck you up!"

"I can't," I sobbed, trying so hard to stop that I caught hiccups.

"Look man, we can't let you go out like this. You want to stay here with us the rest of the day?" Blake asked.

I nodded, and they helped me over to the couch. Malcolm dug around in the side of the sofa cushion and pulled out a half-smoked marijuana blunt. My hands were still shaking as I accepted it from him. Blake lit it, and as I smoked, their hands began to roam my body, catching feels of my most intimate parts.

"Come on, guys!" I protested, choking on the smoke. "You talk about the guys at school feeling my ass and look at you."

"The difference is that you like it when we do it," Malcolm whispered, caressing my ear with his lips, and grabbing my crotch.

I didn't have an argument, especially after him finding that I was as erect as they were.

Blake stood and began to remove his clothes. He looked over his shoulder, sneering seductively as Malcolm and I watched his striptease. His ass tumbled free from his boxers, shiny, black, round, and hairless. He then turned to us, his manhood swinging in its full glory and demanded that we disrobe, too. Malcolm had already begun to pull my shirt off, so all that was left for me to do was undo the shoestring that served as a belt. I stood, and the shorts fell to the floor.

"Goddamn!" Malcolm snickered, taking my manhood in his hands. "You working with all this, and you letting them fools make you their bitch!"

"Is that what you guys want me to be, your bitch? Is that what this is all about?"

"9-11…"

"T'bayo is my name!" I screamed with all the rage I had swallowed since the first time I had heard that awful nickname.

"T'bayo," Malcolm tried again, "all we are trying to do is offer you friendship and protection. We aren't going to use you. In fact, if you want to, put your clothes back on."

I stood, indecisive, looking from him to Blake, searching their faces for the truth. What in the way of friendship did I have to offer two guys like Blake and Malcolm, other than letting them fuck me and copy my homework?

"I don't want to," I swallowed. "I just want you guys to be upfront with me. You don't have to pretend to like me to fuck me, okay?"

"T'bayo, nobody is pretending," Blake promised. "I swear to God that if I had been in the gym when they was doing all that shit to you, it wouldn't have went down that way. They didn't…"

"Rape me?" I finished. "No, they just pissed on me and hit me with leather straps."

"Sounds like German porn," Malcolm laughed, trying to lighten the mood.

"I'm so sorry," Blake whispered, cradling me in his huge arms. I could almost swear I saw a tear forming in his eye before he buried my face against his barrel chest.

I could have stayed there forever, if the feel of Malcolm's tongue, tracing my collarbone, hadn't caused me to turn around. Malcolm then knelt before me again, taking my hard penis into his mouth. Blake followed his lead. Kneeling behind me, he spread my cheeks and his tongue began to trace my rim.

"Oh my god!" I cried out with pleasure.

Malcolm stood and ordered me to take his bright red cock into my mouth. I did and tried not to topple over as Blake commenced to fuck me deeper and deeper with his tongue. I wondered exactly how long and thick his tongue was because it was stretching my rim so wide that it felt like a penis was digging around in me already.

"MMMMM!" he laughed, standing, and began to rub his scorching hot cock against my ass. He then began to smack my cheeks with it, leaving circles of pre-ejaculates all over my skin.

"I'm going to come!" Malcolm moaned and yanked his dick out of my mouth. He grabbed a handful of my hair and pulled my face towards his dick as he jerked out the biggest load of cum I had ever seen in my life.

"Goddamn, man! Already?" Blake laughed. "Looks like it's just more booty for me, then." His hands were on my ass as he spoke, pulling my plump, beige cheeks apart, making them jiggle and bounce as he gently spanked them with his long fingers.

"Go ahead," Malcolm smiled, reaching around to cup my cheeks. "I'll just watch; I'll get a sample later."

"Get a condom!" I demanded, but when I looked over my shoulder I saw that Blake had already beaten me to the punch. His perfectly straight, white teeth were ripping through the rapper of a Magnum.

"You got any Vaseline or anything?" he asked Malcolm. "This boy is either a virgin, or he hasn't been fucked in years," he observed, probing my wet hole with his stubby middle finger.

"Only one time, last year," I confirmed, "so please, don't hurt me! Promise?"

"You know I'm not!" he huffed, pulling the rubber on his throbbing dick as he leaned forward to kiss me. He took a tube of lube from Malcolm at the same time. "Just relax, baby boy. I guarantee you that this is going to feel good for both of us," he promised, smacking my cheeks with his condom-covered thickness.

I could taste the combination of marijuana and my ass on his breath as his tongue played in my mouth. His fingers roamed the crack of my ass, searching blindly for the hole. When he found it, two fingers dug deep, making me wail out in pain.

"Sorry," he promised. "Look, kid, if you don't want to do this, it's fine. We will still be your boys, and we will still protect you. You know that; right?"

"Just don't hurt me," I insisted, kissing him again.

He led me over to the couch, opposite the one that Malcolm occupied, and laid me back. My body sunk in the plush pillows, and it felt as if I was being drowned in velvet. He hoisted my legs up on his shoulders and began to kiss me deeply, passionately, as if he really did have feelings for me.

"Stop!" I pleaded pushing him away. "Don't make me fall in love with you, either. Just fuck me."

"Oh, it's like that?" he huffed, and pushed into my hole with nerve-jolting force.

I cried out in pain, and he apologized again and waited for me to tell him it was okay to proceed. When he did, his thrusts were deep and painful, but not as malicious as his entry.

I knew that I had hurt him by telling him not to make me love him even more so that he had hurt me with his entry.

"Yeah!" Malcolm cheered from the other couch. "Get that pretty ass! Show him how we do the damn thing!"

Blake wasn't interested in showing off for Malcolm, though. His eyes were locked with mine, and it was clear to me that he was still making love to me. I went along with it because he was making me feel so good and kissing me so gently that at that moment I didn't care if he told me that it was all some cruel joke when it was over. Right then and there, he was showing me more love than I had ever experienced, and whether it was real or not, I didn't want it to end.

Malcolm walked over to the couch and stood before me with his dick dangling in my face. I took it into my mouth again. To make my job of sucking easier he climbed on the couch, fucking my face like it was his personal pussy. His ass was in Blake's face as he fed dick down my throat, and I could hear the sound of Blake sucking on Malcolm's rim while he still fucked me, slow and deep.

"Oh fuck yes!" Malcolm moaned. "Eat this ass, Daddy. Damn! Fuck this yellow ass with that tongue!"

"I'm going to do more than just that!" Blake laughed, easing his way from deep in my cavity. He gave each of my thighs a kiss before letting my legs fall flat on the sofa.

He spat on his forefingers and massaged the wetness into Malcolm's rim, then he began to enter him with the greasy condom he had just removed from my ass, much gentler and slower than he had done me just minutes before. If I hadn't been so busy orally pleasuring Malcolm I might have gotten jealous.

"Oh shit! Oh no!" Malcolm moaned. "Damn man, wait! Blake, stop; you know I can't take it all!"

"Be a man about it, dawg! You was just telling me to show T'bayo how we get down."

"Damn, baby – Shit!" Malcolm screamed as Blake crammed the rest of his monster into his tight hole.

I wriggled from under Malcolm to get a better view of the beautiful ordeal. Blake blew me a kiss as I watched him fuck Malcolm so viciously that Malcolm's eyes teared. Malcolm bit the sofa pillows, and when Blake would stab in too deep, he would punch a sofa pillow and curse.

"You like this, T'bayo?" Blake asked, showing off for me. "You want me to fuck you like this next, baby?"

"Hell no!" I laughed. "I was just fine with what you were doing to me at first."

"Damn, Blake!" Malcolm howled. "Why you can't fuck me all gentle and shit, too, like you was doing T'bayo? You sweet on that exotic nigga now? I ain't your boy no more since you got some new booty?"

"You always going to be my nigga, fool!" Blake laughed and slowed down to caress Malcolm's neck and shoulders with his tongue. "There. You like it slow, like this? This how you want this big, daddy dick?"

"Mmm!" Malcolm Purred. "Yeah, Daddy; you can get all this tight ass; just be nice about it." It seemed that he was enjoying the slow pace, and seeing him enjoy it was turning me on much more than seeing him in excruciating pain. I especially enjoyed the view of him jacking off his thick eight inches as Blake stretched him wide and dug him out. The sight of Blake's smooth, chocolate ass, working in circles and glistening with sweat, was icing on the cake.

"I love you," Blake whispered to Malcolm. "Do you believe me?"

"When you fuck me like this, I do!" Malcolm moaned, and then his face contorted. His orgasm came bubbling out, prematurely, again, covering his fist and the sofa pillow beneath him. This time, his cum rushed out with so much force that he trembled and tears began to roll down his face. He turned a bright red and leaned back so he could rest his head on Blake's chest. He began to ride Blake's monstrous ten inches like a mad man. The adrenaline from his orgasm must have made him forget that he was saying he couldn't take it all just minutes earlier.

"Shit, baby! I'm 'bout to nut, too!" Blake moaned, and forced Malcolm back down on his stomach.

He began to fuck him faster and faster, until Malcolm began to cry harder, and tried to crawl away. His attempt at escape was to no avail, as Blake outweighed him by at least twenty pounds of muscle and pressed his torso against Malcolm preventing him from any movement.

"Don't run from me, baby!" he demanded. "I told you I'm about to come; just take it a little bit longer."

"Please bust off!" Malcolm begged under his breath. "It feel like you inside my stomach, punching me, Blake; please come!"

"Alright, baby! Here it comes!" Blake promised snatching out.

He ripped the rubber off, and made a grimace of disgust at the sight of Malcolm's shit and blood. Malcolm still bit the pillow and cried. His sobbing caused his ass cheeks to jiggle as Blake milked forth a flood of white fluids all over hm. It was so much cum that I was glad he hadn't shot off on his face, or poor Malcolm would have drowned.

"You're next," Blake laughed looking at me. "You ready?"

"Please, no!" I begged after seeing the pitiful sight of Malcolm, still slumped over crying. "I don't think I can handle any more today, man. Please don't be mad."

"No, not that," he laughed kneeling between my thighs. "It's your turn to come, boy."

My cock was already swollen well beyond its normal size just from watching them fuck. When he took my shaft into his hands and began to stroke it up and down, teasing the swollen tip with his tongue, I couldn't help but blow a hot wad all over his face.

"Well, goddamn it! I guess we all need to shower again, huh?" he laughed, massaging my cum into his skin.

Lord, please let me have made two new friends, I silently prayed as we walked toward the bathroom, Blake smacking Malcolm's jiggling cheeks with his semi-erect cock, and Malcolm's strong hands prying my cheeks apart to get a glimpse at my twitching hole. I would even settle for only being their pet bitch, but what I couldn't stand was being lonely anymore.

READY OR NOT
By Don Mika

I was eighteen when I lost my virginity to a man. I had only been with one female, and I had given my boyfriend, Omar, many blowjobs. Still, I had yet to let any guy take me all the way. Omar told me that he was okay with the slow pace of our relationship, but there was always something about the look that he got whenever he said that to me that made me question whether or not he would wait around much longer for me to be ready. I decided that my cherry should be his twenty-seventh birthday gift, since I didn't have any money to get him a real present. I also knew that his turning twenty-seven only three days after I had turned eighteen was an omen that he was the one. By that time, I already knew that he cared enough about me to deserve the privilege.

The idea of his huge nine and a half inches prying its way into my tiny opening frightened me to the point of anxiety. If I could survive the entrance of the enormous head, I could get through it, or so I tried to reason with myself. I tried to control my convulsions as he laid me on his bed and began to kiss down my shoulders and back. He and his wife's previous fuck had left the unmistakable stench of his ball's sweat on the sheets, and I became instantly aroused. My heartbeat thundered against the mattress, drowning out his moans and the slurps of his tongue. He commenced licking the top of my cheeks as he ripped my pants all the way down and then began to slide his tongue up and down the length of my crack.

"Relax!" he demanded, as the shock of him inserting a dry finger caused me to jerk in pain. He forced my chest flat against the mattress again. "Take it, baby! You know I wouldn't do nothing to hurt you." His words were muffled by his task of nibbling my cheeks.

"You *are* hurting me," I pointed out as he pushed two big fingers inside me, knuckle-deep. I fought back a scream as he removed them.

"You told me you were ready for all this." He sat on the edge of the bed, taking in deep breaths to control his temper. "If you going to

91

act like a bitch over two little fingers, what you going to do when you get all this dick?"

Something told me that Omar was not going to make good on his promises to take it easy on me. Still, when I looked at the picture of his wife and children on the nightstand, I felt smaller than he could have intended to make me feel with his harsh words, but it wasn't due to what he said. It was because of how immature I was acting. Here I was with a man who had risked losing everything, for the past eight months, just to be with me: his wife and kids, his job as a youth minister, and his position as assistant principal at the local middle school, not to forget his freedom. Enduring a little pain was the least I could do for someone who was willing to jeopardize four years of marriage and risk a jail term just for me.

"I didn't say stop," I attempted to appease him as I rubbed his back. Unfortunately, my hands were too clumsy and shaky to be seductive. "I'm ready for you to fuck me; really, I am, but…"

"There can't be any buts, Jerrin! Fuck it! Just get dressed; I'll just drive you home and go pick up somebody whose sure about if they love me or not! I think you got doubts."

He was even more handsome when he was angry. I definitely had no doubts about wanting to feel those midnight black muscles quiver all over my skinny, yellow torso. I even anticipated the pain of the six-inch circumference of his tip, smashing its way into my ass. At that point, I would have let him have me any way he wanted. I just wanted to know one thing before that happened, just so I would know whether or not to fall completely for him.

"Omar, the other day you said that if the world would accept you and me as a couple, you'd leave your wife and raise your kids with me."

He nodded and sexily arched a thick eyebrow in anticipation of where the conversation was heading.

"Did you mean it?" I finished and cast my eyes to the ground, as I often did whenever I felt that I had stepped over my boundaries in the relationship. I knew that I always sounded stupid to a guy as experienced as Omar.

"I can't believe you're asking me this shit. Not on today of all days, Jerrin! This is my birthday, baby! My wife and the boys are all the way at her mama's house in Florida. You are all I have; please, just let me have you."

"I just want you to tell me the truth!" I shuttered, fighting back nervous tears. "I'm going to let you fuck me either way, but you have to tell me what it means to you; you owe me that."

"Oh, I owe you that? What kind of bullshit is that?" he sort of laughed. I was crushed by the fact that my sincere concerns humored the man that was about to deflower me, but I was aroused by the baritone of his voice and the strength of his strong hands as he grabbed my chin to force me into eye contact with him. "So, you don't believe I love your stupid ass?"

"That's not what I'm saying! Look, this isn't like sucking your dick, Omar! It's going to hurt like hell, and it's going to change me forever. Before I do this, I got to know if you really care about me, or if I'm just the faggot boy down the street, you let suck your dick. I already told you that I'd still let you fuck me either way, so be honest."

He sat silent for a while, and I felt like a complete ass for spoiling the perfect mood. At that moment I completely understood why he never invited me to hang out with his friends whenever he had boys' night. Everything I said made me sound like the stupid kid that I tried to make him forget.

"I know I'm being stupid," I finally spoke. "I'm scared, though, baby."

"I think you're sexy when you're stupid," he teased, sucking the back of my neck. Once again, I was pushed flat on the bed, and he mounted me, grinding his scorching erection against my cheeks. He continued to leave love bites all over my pale torso. I would have to worry about explaining them to my dad later; right now, it felt too good just being underneath the weight of his body.

He positioned my body, rough and demanding, jerking my limbs uncomfortably, until he had me on my knees. My butt was raised enough for him to bury his face between my furry cheeks again. This time he reached under me and began to jerk my dick for me. I twisted my own nipples in response to the pleasure. Once again, his magical tongue was replaced with a finger. This time I bit the sheet to hold in my protest.

"That's right; take it!" he coaxed. "Yeah, you ready for this dick now; ain't you?"

"Yes!" I retorted, willing to withstand anything but the jagged fingernails again.

He flipped me onto my side and hoisted one leg over my shoulder. Spitting on the tip of his penis, he positioned himself for entry: the antagonizing head pressed against my pucker, pulsing and waiting for its chance to rip me open. Pre-ejaculates and saliva allowed just the tiniest portion to slide in, causing me more of a tingle than pain. He held my hands, and we counted together, between kisses, as he prepared to enter on the count of three:

"One... two...

"OOW, shit!" I wailed out because he was too impatient to let me get to three. I started to cry before I could fully process the pain of his jab, and he withdrew, leaning all of his weight against me as he reached for a jar of his wife's hair grease. It was thick and one shade darker black than Omar's beautiful skin. As he rubbed it on my rim, the room became saturated with the smell of pine tar. I wondered if the chemicals in it would burn me, but I would chance it before allowing Omar to enter me again, only using spit.

As I watched him massage some grease on his throbbing, crooked dick, I began to revamp the horror stories I had heard at school: guys getting stuck together and having to be carried out in that condition via ambulance, guys getting torn and having to be stitched up, thereby being called out to the entire world before their proper time. I suddenly wasn't sure I could actually go through with the ordeal. What if Omar got stuck inside me and then the doctors ripped me trying to get us apart? Then I'd be the faggot who got stuck and needed stitches, two walking queer clichés in one.

"Oh, no!" I yelped, feeling him thrust every inch of himself inside of me. All my what-ifs subsided; I was forced to deal with the current pain.

"Don't cry!" he whispered, sticking the two fingers he'd just retrieved from my ass into my mouth to silence my whimpers. The sight and sensation of me sucking his fingers began to turn him on more, and he let me know by going faster, rocking me with each deep thrust, and whispering in my ear that he loved me.

Even love couldn't help me endure the pain. "Stop! Omar, if you love me, stop!" I begged, and as soon as he did, I scrambled from beneath him.

He looked at me with belittling eyes, wiping my blood from his penis, which jerked up and down with excitement. "What now, Jerrin?"

"I think we should be using a rubber." This time I didn't look away. Being the older one, Omar should have been the one suggesting protection. If he thought otherwise, he should have felt as small as he always made me feel when I questioned him. Of course, Omar didn't agree. He looked at me with so much disgust that I wished that I could become a turtle and retract into my shell until his stare ended.

"You think I got something?" he asked, grabbing me so hard that my biceps began to spasm from poor blood circulation. "Look me in my fucking face and tell me that you truly think that I have a disease! How long have you been sucking my dick?"

"If you come in my mouth I can spit it out, but if you come in my ass it's already in my bloodstream; I read that in health. So, do you have a rubber or not?"

He sat, huffing and cursing, for a few seconds; he then went to his bottom drawer and removed a Trojan condom. "Jerrin, my wife counts these! You're starting to make me fuck up!"

"Go to the gas station's vending machine and buy one back when we're done," I suggested. I certainly was worth eight quarters.

"Are you really going to be that silly?" he pouted. "You're the faggot; if anybody should be questioning who might have something it should be me, asking you whose dick you be sucking when you ain't here! I know I don't fuck nobody but my wife!"

"How do I know that? How do you know who she be fucking? And if you let a faggot suck your dick, what does that make you?"

"I'm sorry I said that to you," he whispered tenderly and pulled me toward him. He began to grind against me slowly, making his dick graze mine as we swayed, and he whispered in my ear, between nibbles, that I was his baby. The condom became obsolete at that time. I could have noticed puss boils all over his body, and I still would have licked him from head to toe, and then let him have his way with me. The combination of his deep voice and his strong hands on my ass was always too much to resist.

"You have to trust me," he instructed, placing me on my back this time. My legs were forced over my head, in an uncomfortable position, and my feet were placed against his chest. He twisted my arms above my head and thrust inside me. The pain was intolerable, and he was still only halfway inside of me.

I stopped biting my tongue long enough to beg for a second to adjust, but he was already too far into the ordeal to listen. He began to kiss me, attempting to muffle my screams as he humped in and out of me. Between the weight of his body against mine, and the vicious kisses, almost engulfing my entire mouth, like a cat stealing a baby's breath, I felt like I was dying.

"Yes sir!" he huffed, letting go of my hands. "This pussy sure was worth waiting for! I'd wait another eight months just so it'll feel this good."

I wished I could say the same thing. The only sensation I was feeling was the sting of the pine tar grease, and the force of him slamming in and out of me recklessly. I reached between my thighs, hoping that playing with my dick would take some of the pain away from my ass, but he grabbed my hands again, and they were forced over my head.

"Don't do that, baby. I'm going to make you come," he promised. "I'm going to fuck you so long and deep that you shoot that cum everywhere, without having to touch your own dick."

I had heard of that happening, but I doubted that he could achieve the feat that night. I wasn't enjoying the sensation of him stretching me at all. I sat up and began to suck on his nipples, not knowing what else to do with myself.

"Whoa, easy, baby! Don't do that," he pleaded. "That's going to make me come too quickly. I've been dreaming about this for a long time. Let's just be here together for a while before it's over; you feel me?"

He withdrew from me, and I thanked God aloud. He then inserted his dick into my mouth and straddled me. For the first time, he took my semi-erect penis into his mouth and began to pleasure me back. I was in heaven, until those damn fingers of his found my hole again. This time the feeling was more erotic than painful, and I began to work my hips in slow circles, feeling his fingers dig deeper and deeper into me as we made love to each other's mouths.

Omar sucked my dick like a seasoned pro, taking more of mine in his mouth than I could ever fit of his, but then again, he had me beat by two and half inches. "I'm 'bout to come!" I tried to warn, but he didn't even try to pull away; he went farther down on my dick as my liquids spewed out into his hot mouth. I flapped round on the bed, like a fish out of water, and he stood over me, his eyes smiling at me as he rolled me unto my stomach. Once again, his fingers stretched my cheeks so far apart that I feared my hole would rip. He then spat my load into my hole, and began to spread the mixture of melted sperm and hot saliva with his fingers.

"Damn, baby!" I breathed as he slid his greasy, spit-covered tip across my hole, causing me to buck in pain. He tried to push all of it in too soon. I took a deep breath and bit down on the blanket. It took him longer than the last time to get in, but once he was inside the pain wasn't nearly as severe. I began to enjoy the fullness, the slippery sensation of my sperm and his spit mixing with the grease as he plowed me, but the most gratifying was the smell of his sweat dripping unto my body.

"You want me to hurry up and come?" he teased fucking me harder and faster. "Talk dirty to me and make me come; then I can take all this dick out of your little pussy!"

"I don't know what to say!" I trembled, turning even redder with embarrassment than the pain had caused me to become.

"You know what I want to hear; tell me this is all my pussy!" he demanded, smacking my skinny cheeks so hard that I released tears on the impact. "Tell me I'm the only man you'll ever let get this little, redbone pussy!"

"You know that, Omar!" I begged as he fucked me even harder. "Oh, God, baby, this ass is always going to be yours only; you know that shit!"

"You goddamn right I know that shit' 'cause when I get done with this ass, no other dick is going to be able to touch all your walls at once again! I'm going to stretch this little pussy so that my dick is the only dick that you can ever feel again!"

By then, he was fucking me so viciously that the impact of his nuts and thighs, smacking against my ass with each thrust, echoed through the room, assisting Omar, who had pushed my face in the mattress, in drowning out my screams. His own moans and curses roamed free above my head, and sometimes directly in my ear, whenever he leaned over to dig deeper into me.

"Time out, baby, please! Please give me a minute to catch my breath! Come on, Omar; this shit hurts!" I pleaded as he bounced in and out so hard that the lumpy mattress danced halfway off the bed. Even when I had to balance myself on my fingertips to keep from hitting my face on the marble floor, he continued to fuck me with malice, as if he hadn't just looked in my eyes and told me how much he loved me five minutes earlier. It was as if he was angry with me that he was enjoying himself as much as he was.

"Stop crawling, bitch!" he thundered, smacking my ass so hard that I did actually attempt to jump away from the pain at that moment. I hadn't been crawling at first; he was pounding away at me so roughly that I was sliding off the slippery, satin sheets.

His arms looped under my armpits, and jerk my arms up, and into an inescapable full nelson. Holding me so tight that I couldn't breathe, he stood, and I was forced to stand, too, with his dick still deep inside me. Nothing of me touched the floor but the very tip of my big toes, as I was five-five and Omar was six-two. All I could do was try to work my ass in circles and make him come, so he could stop slamming in and out of me with all his might. On my tiptoes it was a difficult task.

"Stop trying to fuck my dick and let me fuck that ass!" he demanded, squeezing me harder still. He walked us over to the large mirror, and I could see the pain on my face and the ecstasy on his as he fucked me so violently that my legs and my lifeless arms swayed to and fro, making me appear to be an oversized Raggedy Andy with my curly, reddish-brown afro and flushed cheeks.

The pine-tar grease, which he had spooned into my ass earlier, began to melt and trickle down my ass and onto his curved dick and his balls. To me, it looked extremely disgusting, but it appeared to turn him on because he became even more sadistic. Dropping his hold on my arms, he spread my already stretched hole even wider so that he could watch the melted lubricant leak around his dick as he fucked me and grunted, "Yeah! Hell yeah, bitch; take this mutha-fucking dick!" over and over again.

By this point, my hands had fastened around the towel rack, just above the mirror. My feet rested, daintily, against the glass just enough to keep me from falling as he bucked in and out of me, only holding on to my ass.

"I'm gonna come!" he announced, fucking me faster yet.

One deep, unexpected thrust caused me to kick out in pain, shattering the beautiful glass in six pieces. He cursed, and pulled me away before the falling fragments could do any more harm to us than had been caused to my left foot, which was squirting longer and longer jets of blood with each bounce I took against his dick.

I felt him cum deep inside me, and I watched in what was left of the mirror, as the product of his labor leaked out and was pushed back in by his crooked monster over and over, until he couldn't stand the sensation any longer and snatched free from my walls, opening the floodgate for the trapped mixture of red and white juice that bubbled out, mixing with the pool of pine-tar.

"Goddamn it! Baby, you came in me!" I observed, in terror.

He smiled in response. Leaving a trail of bloody semen and tar behind, he toted me to the shower, and held the injured leg up for me, backing me against the wall and pushing his dick inside me again, he began to urinate in me, and tried to convince me that it would kill any infection. Of course, I wasn't buying it, but the sensation of the hot liquids against my throbbing walls was so phenomenal that I went along with it.

"Don't take it out!" I begged as he sucked my neck and twisted my nipples. All the while, his hot piss sloshed around inside my cavity, only leaking out in tiny droplet at a time. I grew so hot that I felt faint, and thanked God that he was holding my thigh, and that I was supporting myself against the shower walls on my fingertips, or I would have smashed my face when my spring of cum burst forward from my dick, painting his rippled abs. He hadn't lied after all; he did make me come without having to touch my dick. Regretfully, that was the first and last time that anyone would accomplish that feat.

"Here I go again!" he screamed, removing his cock. "I'm gonna nut again!"

My ass made a sound like a plunged drain, and his piss shot out. He tried to stop the flood with his dick, which was erupting with its own hot larva. Finally, he gave up and fell against me, forcing my back so hard against the shower that I lost my breath.

"I really do love you, Jerrin," he whimpered, when we were both able to speak again, "so don't ever doubt that shit again, especially not to my face!"

"I love you, too, Omar!"

I shuttered at the feel of the shower stream, and melted at the feel of his sweet lips against mine, and at the sensation of his hands soaping my body up ever so gently. I wished at that moment that my parents' curfew couldn't make our night come to an end in less than twenty minutes.

CALL ME CRAZY
By Don Mika

So, I'm lying here, butt-ass-naked, watching this chocolate god play dress-up in my brand new $230 jeans and matching jacket, and it occurs to me that I didn't even catch his goddamn name. I hope it begins with D, seeing as how he has a big ass capital D branded all over the back of his neck. Shit, maybe the big D is his way of advertising; if so, he certainly told the truth. Trust me, nothing under eleven inches gets into my wardrobe.

"I look scraight in this?" he asks, throwing the jacket open to reveal the most perfect six-pack. The waist of the jeans sags low enough to show the start of his silky pubic hairs.

Thank god he had the decency to stay the fuck out of my underwear.

Damn, "scraight" is an understatement. He doesn't know how tempted I am to run my tongue across the place where his hip joint meets his abs.

"You look all right in that, but I liked the black outfit much better."

"I ain't tried on nothing black!"

"I meant the wet, black suit you had on when you stepped out of the shower."

"Oh," he shrugs, and steps forward before I can kiss the back of his neck. He proceeds to cram his size twelve and a half feet into my size ten and a half Timbs (also unworn).

It's funny how my sexual advances seemed to disgust him much less yesterday, when I found him wondering up and down the street: in the rain, drunk as shit, and mumbling about how he had fucked things up with his bitch and didn't have a place to lay his head. Still, I'm not the least bit upset by his behavior. I've dealt with straight guys before. I know he'll be right back in my bed as soon as he goes home, fucks the hell out of his girl, and realizes that what he's done to me didn't take the ability or desire to fuck her away from him. Once he bust off inside of his bitch, our thing will be tighter than the Virgin Mary's twat. The trick is waiting. A sissy with no patience and too much pride always loses a good piece of dick.

"Hey...yo, Pa, I just want to let you know that I thank you for taking me in last night and shit. I promise I'm gon get this gear back to you, too."

"Keep it" I shrug, already aware that he has every intention of doing so. But, Mama didn't raise no fool. There is still a chance that I won't ever see this nigguh again once he pimps his pretty ass out my door.

Did I neglect to mention that I gave him thirty bucks for cab fair? Best believe I'm getting a third helping of that chocolate bar!

"What you doing?" he chuckles in discomfort, as my hands tug at the belt to the jeans. "Look, for real yo … it don't feel right this morning. I ain't high enough, or something!"

Oh, that's classic! He has to be high, huh? Well, I don't know why he's sober anyway. I gave him sixty-five dollars to scoop up a quarter of kind-bud from my boy down the street two hours before we last fucked, and it has only been two hours since. Now that bag is empty, and I don't even smoke weed! I can't lie, though; a bitch did get horny off the contact.

"Let me make you high," I whisper, kneeling to tickle his bellybutton with my tongue. That seemed to be his spot the night before.

He stands, indecisive and huffing for a few seconds before he nods and says, "Shit! Go ahead, but you better fuckin' hurry up! I ain't trying to get in trouble with my girl again, fucking with you, over some bullshit like this!"

The nerve of this mutherfucker! Like I'm in total control of how fast his kids swim to the opening of his dick!

I unzip his pants, and his hard dick jumps out, hitting me right on the forehead. One of his hands wraps around the rack on my closet door, and the other fidgets around in his pocket for a cigarette – or anything that will take his attention away from the fact that a man is giving him the best head of his life. Once his cigarette is lit, he cast his head towards the ceiling, as if he can't bear to look, and palms my head like a basketball with the free hand, forcing my mouth to take the black mass of veins into my throat before my eyes can finish devouring it. The feeling of his big head scraping the sides of my jaw turns me on to the point that I struggle to pump my cock, but he is fucking my throat so fast and viciously that if I don't keep my hands locked behind his knees, we will lose our balance.

When he finally lets me come up for air, I see his stomach heaving and notice that he has worked up quite the sweat. Droplets cascade from ripple to ripple, shining his black skin like Pledge wiped on a wooden table, enticing me to taste him.

I do.

"Stop bullshitting and suck it!" he demands, grabbing the sides of my face in his powerful right hand. The other one feeds his pole into my mouth. He continues to bang away at my tonsils. After a few more minutes of brutally gagging me with it, he takes it out, and smacks my face with it, leaving a film of spit and precum sliding down my jaw. I struggle to lick it away, but my tongue is too short to reach it. He enters my mouth again, now holding the back of my head with both hands. My neck feels as if it's going to break, because he's bobbing my head up and down for me.

Damn, this thug ass nigga is making my dootie-hole throb and ache to be filled! Fuck this blowjob shit! I know what I want, and I've dealt with guys like him long enough to know how to get it, just the way I want it.

I push his hands away and stare up at his questioning eyes as I attempt to stand to my feet. His hands seize my head, preventing me from rising.

"What the fuck is you doing, yo?" he asks.

"I'm through!"

"What the fuck you mean you through, nigguh?" He waves his cock before my face, gliding it across my lip like a tube of lip-gloss. I fight with myself not to let the feel of pre-cum weaken me and make me open my mouth.

"No!" I say, pushing his hands away again. This time, I stand before he can grab me.

"Bitch, you better stop goddamn playing!"

"I'm not playing. Your girl is expecting you in an hour. It's hard as hell to get a cab around this part! Your best bet would be to leave now."

"Bitch, how the fuck you gon ..." he rushes towards me with his fist clenched, his heavy dick swinging. He stops halfway to take in a deep breath. "Look man, you can't just get me rock like this, slob all up on my shit, and tell me to leave, now! Be fair! What you think I'm s'posed to do, use my dick to wave a cab down?"

I'd certainly stop and pick up anybody waving a dick that big and pretty at my Lexus. Anyway, I digress.

"I just don't feel right doing this." I struggle to keep the laugh from bursting forth as I spit the lie out. It certainly is fun to turn the tables. "You got a wife and a son! You been talking all morning about how you can't wait to get home and play with your baby!"

"Well, they ain't here, and you need to keep my family out of this shit!" The demanding look in his eyes as he points to the brick swinging between his thighs tempts me to crawl forward, like the bitch I am, and obey my master, but I have to be strong to get my money's worth. "You giving up some head or some ass, one!" he screams rushing towards me again. This time he hits me, much harder than I could ever anticipate, and I fall backwards. My legs spread wide, giving him the perfect view of the place he yearns to dwell, as I crawl backwards and beg him not to do to me what I truly desire. I look above my head at the source of the verbal bashing, and see him struggle to pull a condom unto his curved dick while he undoes a bottle of lube with his perfectly white and straight teeth.

"Get your bitch ass on that bed!" he screams kicking me hard, though I make prompt efforts to obey his commands. "Hurry the fuck up, too, nigguh! Ain't nobody playing with you!"

The blow to my temple has my vision so distorted that I see three big dicks pulse before me as I heave myself unto the bed with my legs spread-eagle. He mounts me, struggling to cram all of himself into my tiny opening at once. Lust has him oblivious to the fact that he is ruining my $300 sheets, and my outfit, with his greasy handprints. As he rips the jacket off and throws it behind him, he leaves the jeans dangling at his ankles. "Shut the fuck up!" he screams, covering my mouth and nose with his huge hand. He makes an odd face, as if he's summoning some inner force, then jabs the remaining eight inches so far inside of me that my hips raise up from the bed in shock. He then permits, and even demands, that I make noise. "That's right; scream, you punk ass bitch! You know you can't take all this dick! Scream like the bitch you is!" His hand slaps my face as he fucks me into a soprano note. "Say you a bitch, nigguh! Say you my fuckin bitch! Say it, or I'll fucking kill you!"

"OH SHIT! I'm a bitch ... ass ... nigguh! I'm your bitch! OH FUCK! Ouch!"

He laughs and hoists my legs so far up that my toes scrape the headboard as he fucks me harder and deeper. His hands fasten around my ankles, pushing my knees to my chest, restricting my movement and breathing. I love every second of it, especially his deep voice as he tries to humiliate me. Little does he know that all I need is a second dick, fucking my mouth, and I would be in sissy-heaven.

"Who the fuck you thought you was playing with?" he screams over my groans of pain, and I watch in the mirror as he balances himself on his tiptoes and knuckles.

Yes! This thug ass nigguh is doing pushups in the pussy!

I contemplate stretching the cramps out of my thighs, but he hits really hard, and that fact frightens me as much as it turns me on. I decide to reach around and support the back of my knees with my hands instead of putting my thighs down.

"You gon have a period when I get finish with this ass!" he grunts, forcing my thighs even wider, and I am convinced that he is not making an idle threat.

"Please stop! I can't take no more!" I beg, fully aware of the consequences.

He doesn't disappoint me. "I know you ain't say stop!" he roars, driving so deep into me that I inch backwards, wrenched with pain. My head hits the headboard, and he continues to fuck me so fast and viciously that I can't help but break into tears as I watch us in the mirror over my bed. I reach between our torsos and begin jerking my dick, which he has bent uncomfortably against his stomach. I watch his coal-black ass glisten with sweat as it flexes and works in fast circles, sending his colossal dick in and out of my battered hole.

Each time he wriggles a few inches out, I watch the cheeks of his ass spread, revealing a sexy patch of curls and a beautiful chocolate swirl, and my mind sets my hand to milking my seven inches faster. I imagine how good it might feel if he were to allow me to enter that swirl, just as he forced his way into mine, but the fact that he never will excites me the most.

I can hear his heart beat and feel the veins in his cock pulse against the inner walls of my ass. I know that he will come soon, so I speed up my task of masturbating, determined to come while he is still tangible. Trust me, once guys like D bust off, they don't stick around to make sure you get your next breath, let alone a nut.

"UMMMPh! UMMMPH! Just like pussy!" he grunts, slamming in and out of me so fast that my bed begins to dance across the floor. Don't get me wrong, my bed has had so much wear and tear that one leg is slightly shorter than the rest, so it is easy to make it move, but D is the only fuck-buddy I have had make it travel the entire foot and seven inch distance from the boarder of my Oriental rug and the wall.

Now with the bed against the wall, he pushes my legs so far over my head that my toes scrape the walls, too. I am no longer able to stroke my dick in this position, and I don't have to. His thick dick is putting just the right amount of pressure on my prostate to send my milky whiteness flying out all over his sweaty chest and stomach.

"You nasty mutha-fucka!" he screams, slapping me so hard that he puts an end to my chills of ecstasy. I quickly regain the sensation as I see my sperm mix with his sweat and drip unto my body. His face contorts with anger, at the feel of my sperm dripping down his skin, but he never stops fucking me, even when his hands fasten around my throat. "You nasty bitch! I should fuckin kill you!" he screams, fucking me harder and faster yet, his hands still around my neck.

After minutes of begging him to spare my ass and my life, he releases his hold on my neck and snatches free from my tunnel, peeling the condom from his dick. "Your faggot ass likes to cum on people, huh?!" he breathes, straddling my face. By wrapping one strong hand around the back of my neck, he savagely jerks my face towards his dick. The other hand works so fast, pumping his dick that it occasionally slips off, hitting me hard in the nose or lip and making me question if it is a mistake. He releases his hold on the back of my neck long enough to smack my head as he curses. "Your sorry ass just gon fucking cum on me, like I'm your bitch! Nigguh, what the fuck is wrong with you?"

The free hand then fastens, steadfast to my neck again, and I feel the huge head of his penis force into my lips, which are already cracked and dry from my screaming, and from biting them to hold in screams. I can't see it, but I taste his salty, hot concoction as it flies into my throat, almost making me choke. I become increasingly angry as I feel him release more and more of it down my throat. I don't feel that I have done a good job unless I have to wash at least one-third cup of sperm from my baby smooth face. From the feel of things, he had just shot a half-cup into my stomach, and I couldn't see one drop.

"Whew!" he trembles from head to toe, withdrawing from my lips and shaking the final drops of orgasm unto my face as if he'd just pissed and was voiding leftover urine. To further humiliate me, he smears it with the tip of his penis. He makes me lick the last drop from the tiny crevice, and my dick begins to harden again with excitement.

I slouch down on the bed, shaking with tears of pain and pleasure, as I watch him redress. He notices the grease stains on my unworn suit and peels it off, throwing it to the ground. It is replaced with a new Sean Jean jogging suit, and the Timbs are kicked across the room and replaced with my new pair of matching Jordan's.

The way he smiles as he poses in the mirror proves that we both think he looks twice better in that outfit. He turns around to see if I am asleep, and, of course, I pretend to be. I lie motionless as I hear him dig around in my drawer for the $150 that he watched me stash earlier.

Call me crazy, but he deserves it. I haven't had sex that good since I was seventeen and had spent the night in jail for stealing gay pornography from a local bookstore (thank God that my parents were so embarrassed that they refused to bail me out, but, again, I digress).

My heart speeds up as I see him snatch my extra house key from the hook and tuck it into his crotch as he exits. Even with shoes two sizes too small, he still has the sexiest strut in the world. I don't worry about him having my key. That just gives me hope of seeing him again, which is more than I can say about the many others. Whether he returns to rob or ravish me again, I will be here, waiting for him.

SEEDED IN THE BIG EASY
By Donald Webb

Donald Webb has had short stories published in numerous gay magazines and anthologies. He lives with his life-time partner in Victoria, BC. andon402@shaw.ca

It's midnight when I walk into the backroom bar. I've heard stories about the bar, but they haven't prepared me for the uninhibited scene before me. Every conceivable sexual act is occurring right before my eyes. I'm sure the bar is air-conditioned, but the fresh air doesn't reach the backroom. I can feel sweat beginning to dampen my tight Tee as I work my way through the pack of horny numbers. The place has the grungy smell of a locker-room full of sweating football players, heightened by the distinctive aroma of leather and amyl.

I'm sipping a beer, leaning against the wall, taking in the sights, when the person next to me speaks. It's so dark I have to move in close to see him. He's a stunning African-American. His beautiful white teeth sparkle in the dim light.

"Huh?" I say.

"You're gorgeous," he says in a southern drawl.

I can feel a slight increase in my pulse as I gaze into his obsidian eyes. "My name's Cory," I say, offering him my hand.

His hand is big, warm, and firm. "Daniel," he says.

"You from New Orleans?" I ask.

He shakes his head. "No, Natchez ... and you?"

"On vacation ... from Kansas."

He moves his hand and covers my semi-hard dick. "You havin' a good time?"

"Am now," I answer, as I grope his basket, "how 'bout you?"

"Better now," he says as he places his beer on a shelf and pulls me into his arms. His mouth covers mine, and his hands grip my ass-cheeks. I can feel his hard-on pressing against mine. The manly scent emanating from his body is intoxicating. I gasp when his hand slides into the back of my Levi's and his finger probes my sweaty hole. I suck his tongue when it slithers into my mouth. I can smell my butt on his finger when he brings it up to our noses. "Nice," he says as he licks his finger.

He loosens my Levi's and push them down my thighs. I'm not wearing briefs, so my naked ass is out in the open for all to see. A hand reaches out of the darkness and fondles my butt. Daniel spreads my ass-cheeks. I groan when a wet tongue laps my exposed pucker. Daniel allows the guy to rim me for a few minutes then he pushes him away and shoves his finger into my tight hole. I've only ever fooled around with guys my own age, and only fingers have violated my ass, so I'm basically still a virgin. A real man has never dominated me, but I'm enjoying every move he makes. I'm so turned-on, if he wants to fuck me, right there, in front of everyone, I'll let him do it.

Daniel continues with the ass play for a while, and then he whispers in my ear. "You have a crib?" He sees the look of confusion in my face. "A place where we can go? I like foolin' 'round in here – but I wanna get you in the sack."

I think it's over. I've never taken a stranger home with me, and I've heard about the bad things that can happen, especially in New Orleans, but I want to see what it feels like to be fucked by a real man – after all, that's why I came here – so I acquiesce. "Yeah. I'm staying in a hotel on Bourbon – you wanna come over?"

"That sounds great."

I pull up my Levi's, we finish our beers, then we head for my hotel. I'm a little apprehensive when we enter the lobby – scared that we'll be challenged, but there's no one behind the desk, so I rush him up the stairs.

"Okay if I take a shower?" he asks when we enter my room.

The raunchy scent emanating from his body is a real turn-on, but I'm too shy to tell him, so I say, "Sure."

I'm naked and under the sheets when he comes out of the bathroom. I watch as he dries his hair. There isn't an ounce of fat on his six-foot frame. His well-developed biceps and pecs ripple as he moves his arms. His long dick swings back and forth like a pendulum when he approaches the bed. It stiffens up and the big knob points in my direction, so I roll over and suck him into my throat, all the way in, right to his pubes.

"Oh yeah, baby," he says. "It's been a long time since I had that done to me."

I can't believe it. A gorgeous sensuous hunk like him must have to fight off the guys. He lets me suck him for a few minutes then he moves on top of me – planting his lips on mine, slipping his tongue inside my mouth. He licks my neck and armpits. I watch as he works his way down my torso. He stops to lick my navel, and then he moves further down and sinks my hard-on into his mouth. He sucks for a while, then he pushes my legs up to my chest, and attacks my manhole like he's coming off a long diet.

His face is wet with saliva and ass juice when he comes to his knees between my legs and places his swollen knob at the entrance to my chute. I back away and reach for the lubricant in the bedside table.

"Take it easy," I say as I prepare my hole. "This is new to me."

He lubricates his shaft and places the head at the entrance to my channel. I expect pain – and there is some – but I'm overcome with pleasure when he slides all the way in, opening me up wider and deeper than I've ever been before. He grabs my ankles and pounds my rear-end, giving it the kind of action that I've long dreamed about.

I hook my legs behind my arms, completely opening myself to him, and then I grab my dick and jerk-off in time to the jackhammering of my prostate. I can tell he won't last long. His eyes close, his head arches backwards, and then he lets out a long wail. "Oh fuck, baby, I be comin'... shoot your load."

I grab my nuts with my free hand and squeeze them in my fist as my dick explodes, spurting cum over my chest and face. He licks the cum off my body, then brings his mouth to mine. When his tongue enters my mouth, I can taste my own cum. His dick, still bone hard, continues to probe my chute. "It's been a long time since I fucked anyone," he whispers in my ear. "I'm still hard. Can you feel me up there?"

"I sure can," I say as I milk him with my newly deflowered channel. I never want the incredible feeling to end. He can fuck me all night if he wants.

I'm disappointed when he pulls his cock out my hole, and says, "I want to see your butt, roll over." I expect him to throw it back into me when I'm face down, but he surprises me when lowers his mouth and felches his cum from my hole. He pulls me to my knees and fucks me like a dog. I can feel his sweat dripping on my back. This session lasts much longer than the first, and by the time he shoots his load, my chute feels raw. I don't come; his deep probing is satisfying enough for me.

Thoroughly exhausted, we drift off to sleep. The next morning I wake to the sound of the door closing. He's walking towards the bathroom. "What's happening?" I ask.

"Sorry, didn't mean to wake you. I just puttin' out the, 'Do Not Disturb' sign. I'm gonna take a shower."

I'm languidly stroking my dick when I turn on the television, and tune-in to *Headline News*. I'm only vaguely interested in the news – I'm more interested in getting plowed again – but then I'm jolted wide-awake when a photograph appears on the screen and the announcer says, "The hunt for Philip Grant, the thirty-six-year-old death-row inmate, who escaped while being transferred to New Orleans, continues. Police are asking the gay community in New Orleans for their help after Grant was seen in The Dungeon last night. They assume that he picked up someone last night and went home with him. The police are warning that Grant is extremely dangerous. If you see Grant; do not attempt to approach him, call 911."

There's no doubt that the person they're discussing is in my bathroom. What can I do? I turn off the television, but it's too late. Daniel – or whatever his name is – is standing in the bathroom doorway. "So now you know. Don' be gettin' no ideas. If you do what I say, then you be okay."

I can't concentrate on what he's saying – I have to get out of there. I jump out of the bed and rush for the door. He's a lot quicker than I. Before I get halfway to the door his muscular arms circle my chest, and a hand clamps over my mouth. "Now listen to me, very carefully," he says. "I don' want to hurt you, but I'll kill you if I have to. I done it before, and don' have nothin' to lose. You got that?" When I don't answer, he repeats more forcefully, "You got that?"

This time I nod.

"Let me explain what's gonna happen. You and me are gonna get dressed and walk out of here. When we get out of the city, I'll let you go unhurt, but only if you do exactly what I say. You understand?"

I nod again.

"Come into the bathroom with me."

We enter the bathroom. He stands behind me. As I watch in the mirror, I hear a sharp clicking noise, and then one of his arms holds me tight as the other holds a switchblade knife to my throat. I gasp when he slowly runs the blunt side of the knife over my Adam's apple. He hasn't had time to shower, so I can smell his sweating body. His breath is hot in my ear, when he whispers, "All I got to do is turn the blade over and you a goner."

I can hardly breathe when he slowly runs the flat side of the blade down my chest, pausing briefly at my nipples, and then on to my dick. His erect dick slides back and forth between my moist ass-cheeks. My dick lengthens and rises. The head slides out of my foreskin when he touches it with the knife blade. My mind's in a whirl. What's wrong with you? He's threatening you with death, and yet you want him more than ever.

"They say I killed him in cold blood, but that ain't true. It were his fault. If he listened to me, he'd be alive."

His words don't still my racing heart.

He bends me over the vanity, and then drops to his knees behind me. His unshaven face scratches my tender butt when his tongue probes my chute. I should resist but I can't ... I want to be dominated by him. "Fuck me," I say. "Give it to me."

"Don' move," he says.

He walks into the bedroom and returns with the lube. He doesn't know it, but this time I'm so turned on I would let him fuck me without lube. I watch in the mirror as he lubes his dick. He slaps my butt a few times and then, with one shove, plants his root deep inside me. He places the knife on the vanity, grabs my hips, and pounds my rear-end. I clamp down on his rod when I feel his cum exploding in my chute. Cum erupts spontaneously from my dick, landing on the vanity mirror when he pulls me upright.

We stand like that for a moment, then he slowly withdraws his dick and says, "You got five minutes to wash and dress."

When I come out of the bathroom, he's dressed in some of my clothes, opening and closing the switchblade, making me more nervous than ever. "Move it," he commands.

116

I quickly slip into the clothes I'd worn the night before. They smell gross, but I don't care. He throws me my car keys, and then drapes a jacket over his arm to cover the knife. "Let's go. Remember what I said. I ain't got nothin' to lose. One false move, and you dead."

"What about my clothes?"

"Fuck your clothes; bring the lube."

I can feel the knife digging into my back as we make our way downstairs. I think of screaming, but I know that would be fatal. By the time we're in my car I'm resigned to my fate. He makes me drive, giving me directions, holding the knife out in the open so that I can see the sunlight glinting on the shiny blade. We head west on the I-10.

Nervousness makes me drive too fast. "Slow down!" he yells. "Use the cruise control."

"Where we going?" I ask.

"California," he says.

We're in New Mexico, and I'm beginning to tire. He must have sensed this because he says, "Take the next exit. It's time to find a place to sleep." We're driving down a secondary road, on the outskirts of a small town, when he says, "That place look good."

I look in the direction he's pointing. It's a small farmhouse, some distance from the road. "What are you going to do? What if they call the cops?"

"They better do exactly what I tell them, or they gone."

I drive slowly up the long driveway – watching for signs of life, but the place is quiet. He pushes me toward the front door, and then rings the bell. I can hear the chimes echoing through the house, but there are no other sounds – the place seems deserted. He stoops down and peers through the mail-slot. "They not here. Drive 'round the back."

We stash the car behind the house. He smashes a small glass window in the backdoor with the handle of his knife then pushes his arm in and opens the door. I'm really nervous once we're inside, but I can see by the dust that the place is empty. He drags me from room to room and then back to the kitchen. "Gimme the keys," he says. "I don' wan' you doin' nothin' you'll regret."

I toss him the keys.

"Check the cupboards. I'm hungry," he says.

I find some canned stew and beans and empty them into pots. After we've eaten, we head upstairs to the main bedroom. He pulls the bedclothes down then says, "Okay, get your clothes off."

While I'm stripping, he's looking through the closets and drawers. "Well, well. Ain't this nice."

I look on in horror when he pulls a small handgun from a drawer and loads it. "Just what I need."

When we're naked on the bed, he pulls me on top of him, holds me in a bear hug, and then clamps his lips to mine. I'm immediately hard, once again overcome with lust. He runs his hands down to my rump and fingers my asshole.

"I wan' you to fuck me," he says.

"What? You want me to ..."

"You heard me. I wanna see what it feels like. I wanna feel your cock in me. Who knows ... I might never get the chance again. I wan' you to make love to me."

I tentatively begin exploring his torso with my tongue – more aroused than I have ever been before. The scent of his masculine body, and his taste, acts like an aphrodisiac on me. I raise his arms, lick his pits, and then move my mouth over his smooth chest to his small nipples. He groans in lust as I gently chew on the small tabs of flesh.

I move down his body until his hard dick confronts me. I can smell my own juices on him. I tongue the head of his cock and then move it into my mouth, deep-throating him, rubbing his nuts against my chin. He lets me pleasure him for a while then he pushes me off his dick and raises his legs to his chest. I rim his furry virgin hole.

"Enough," he suddenly says. "I wan' you in me."

My hand is shaking when I pull the lube out of my pants pocket. I smear lube onto my dick and slowly push it into his tight hole. He grabs my butt and jerks me into him. He's so tight, that I feel pain as I enter him. He lies still for a few moments with his eyes closed. "Fuck me hard. I wan' you to come inside me," he eventually says. "I wish you could start a new life in me. That way I be havin' a piece of you with me."

As I piston my dick in and out his silky chute, he seems to be a totally different person. The hardness that I witnessed during the day is no longer evident. He's passive and loving as I fuck his virgin hole. It's not long before I'm shooting my load deep inside his core. He quickly unseats me and rolls me onto my stomach. His dick is lubed and up my channel in record time. It takes only a moment for him to reach an orgasm.

He ties my arm to his, then rolls over and falls asleep. I think briefly of escape, but deep down I know I want to stay with him, so I snuggle up next to him and fall into a deep sleep. The next morning we are once again on the I-10, only this time he's driving. We stop for gas and snacks.

We've been driving for a while when he suddenly says, "Don' turn around. We got company."

I slouch down in the seat and look in the side mirror. "Oh, God, it's the cops. What're we going to do?"

"We ain't doin' nothin'. Take it easy. We wait and see what he does."

We continue driving for a while, and then the lights begin to flash on the cruiser. Daniel doesn't stop. He presses his foot down on the accelerator, and we take off. "Fasten your seatbelt," he says, as he moves the gun from under the seat and tucks it into his waistband.

I'm terrified. I'm a law-abiding citizen, I've never been in trouble, and yet I'm in a car, chased by a cop, while abetting a death-row inmate. Things sure have changed. We're doing over 100 miles an hour when Daniel decides to exit the freeway. He's going much too fast for the sudden bend in the off-ramp. The car becomes air-borne, and then we're rolling down an embankment. Time seems to stand still, as though things are happening in slow motion. We roll a good 100 yards before the car, in a cloud of dust, comes to a stop on the driver's side.

I'm unhurt – the airbags have deployed, but Daniel, who was not wearing his seatbelt, is bleeding profusely from a wound on his forehead. He looks up at me and says, "Thanks for the ride. Now go – quickly, before the cops get here."

In shock, I loosen the seatbelt and begin to move. "Wait!" he says. "Kiss me before you go."

I wipe the blood from his mouth and kiss his cold lips. "Go now," he says.

I climb out of the passenger door and lower myself to the ground. As I move away from the car I hear the sound of a gunshot. I'm hysterical as I run towards the cop. "Put your hands on your head," he yells.

Even though I'm in shock I obey his command. When I reach him, his gun is pointing at my chest. He quickly frisks me then places me in the rear of the cruiser. "Are you Cory Webster?" he asks. When I nod yes, he asks, "Is Philip Grant in the car?" I nod again. He picks up his radio, "Webster's safe, I've got him in the cruiser, but Grant is still in the car."

I must've passed out for a while because I suddenly realize that there are cruisers all around and a paramedic is checking me out. "You're lucky to be alive," she says.

"What about ...?" I can't finish the question.

"You mean Grant?" a cop asks.

"Yeah. Is he ...?"

"Dead? Yeah, the fucker shot himself. I guess he couldn't tolerate the thought of going back to death-row."

I feel like bawling, but I maintain my cool.

Later on the police tell me the desk clerk recognized Grant when we were leaving, so he called the police. They checked the room for fingerprints. When the prints turned out to be Grant's, they issued an APB for my car.

The headlines the next day relate how a mad killer kidnapped me in New Orleans and then nearly killed me in the car accident. Of course, I keep my mouth shut. How can I describe how I really felt about him? Who would believe that for a brief period I had really loved him?

I still think about him from time-to-time. It was the most erotic episode of my life, and I'll never forget it.

ROCK-HARD HANDSOME
By R. W. Clinger

R. W. Clinger has numerous books and stories published through STARBooks Press. He can be reached by e-mail: kenitorico@verizon.net.

1 – MAKE YOU CREAM

It isn't fair how rock-hard handsome Jamar Louis is: six-two frame, skin the color of midnight oil, pearly white teeth, firm jaw, amber-colored eyes, muscles out the wazoo, abs of steel, twenty-six-years-old, and a cock the size of the Eifel Tower. The guy is French, black, and beautiful all the way. He's in New York City for just a short visit from his native land, spending approximately a week with me in my apartment. As every day slips by, I cannot remove my eyes from his delectable skin, his adorable grin, and the tenderness he seems to reek of, both inside and out.

A friend of mine named Lincoln has lined him up to crash at my place. All this goes down rather quickly: Jamar is a well-known photographer; he's in the city to take pictures of some super-hot black baseball star in a pair of Underling underwear; the shoot is tomorrow near 20 Rock. Lincoln insists that Jamar bunks with me, knowing I have a spare room. Jamar explains that he likes to bunk with strangers. before I realize what happens, he spends a night at my apartment, two nights, and decides to inhabit my queer world for the next week.

Sexy as hell. This is what I surmise about the photographer. Too good to be true gorgeous. Someone who should be in front of the camera instead of behind it. I lick my lips every single moment I take his spectacular body in: sweaty biceps, rigid abs, thick thighs, tangles of black hair under his comma-shaped navel. With much adoration and bliss, I find myself playing with my eight-inch tool when he's not around, stroking juice out of the throbbing shaft and decorating my Jamaican skin with sticky-white splotches of Justice Tine-goo. When he's around, though, I'm well-behaved, a complete gentleman and host.

Once, he checks me out from head to toe. I climb out of the shower and dash to the linen closet for a fresh towel in the hallway between our bedrooms. The guy sits on his bed, playing on his laptop. His bedroom door is wide open and ... he studies my chocolate-colored body like a Google map: five-eleven bulk, basketball playing-induced muscles on my arms and legs, sprigs of hair between my ripped pecs, ladder-like chest, pointed nipples, crystal blue eyes, magazine-perfect crew cut, and an ear-to-ear grin that sets the mood.

Purposely, I hang at the closet for an extra amount of time, showing the temporary guest everything I have to offer him: five limp and uncut inches off dark hose between my legs, swinging balls covered in tangles of spiral man-hair, and a thatch of zebra-black V-hair above my crank.

Truth is, Jamar looks quite hungry for a coffee shop owner such as I. His eyes never stray from my tools. Instead, I actually witness him licking his lips, and toying with his jean-covered package between his legs with his left hand. Rather forwardly, he asks, "Looking for something, Just?"

I'm looking for the man of my dreams. Mr. Right to spend the rest of my life with. A French photographer to blow me before he has to leave to do whatever he's here to do in our hefty-sized city. Instead of mentioning these prominent responses, I simply say, "A towel."

He teases me and says in French from the spare bed, "You don't need a towel with a body like yours."

I'm a little rusty with my French and tell him thanks for the compliment. Honestly, it sounds more like Texan cowboy than Parisian, black seducer.

To my surprise, Jamar sets his laptop on a nearby night stand, climbs off the queen-sized bed, adjusts the mound of protein-filled denim between his hulking legs, and rattles off in his thick accent, "Here, let me help you."

Before I can respond, the sexy black god stands behind me. His middle presses against my bare bottom as he reaches around me for a towel; there's a stack of cotton directly in front of me, which I have purposely ignored. While he pulls down a towel from the stack, collecting it at my rippled chest, he brushes his furred chin against the right side of my neck, and whispers, "You knew it was there the entire time, my friend."

"I did, didn't I?" I respond, gasp for oxygen, and feel light-headed because of his utter closeness.

The photographer laughs behind me, brushes his tongue against my neck, breathes my freshly washed black skin into his lungs, and admits, "I like dark-skinned Americans."

"Naked ones, I'm sure."

"Naked ones are the best." His right hand falls down to my navel, brushes against its taut skin, quickly pulls away, and he adds, "Black is the color of sexy. I want to photograph you."

Cream actually leaks out of my semi-hard shaft between my legs. Thank God I have the cotton towel covering my goods, collecting the pre-spew in its fabric instead of dripping to the hallway's wooden floor.

"Soon … I take pictures of you."

I laugh and admit, "A photographer's sloppy seconds in front of his camera, huh?"

Jamar doesn't get my joke. Besides, he's far too interested in licking the side of my neck and pushing his fingertips and palm under cotton and into my patch of bristly knob-hair. Now, he finds exactly what he's looking for and wraps fingers around my semi-inflated beef, which he strokes up and down once … twice … three times.

"Jamar," exits my mouth as I close my eyes. My right hand drops the towel to the hallway's floor, reaches for the closet's oak frame, and holds up my weight.

"Make you cream," he confesses in a matter of seconds between licks, and applies bites to my arched neck. "Make you shoot on the floor," he adds, sharing simple laughter behind me.

My last boyfriend was Arjun Luc, a Jamaican like me, about ten months ago. Sex was not imperative for the man, and I ended up dumping his ass. Truth is I haven't been with a man since, tend to jerk off with black porn, and …

Jamar cranks my beef into life. Five inches grow into six inches … seven inches … eight inches, and he plays with it for a few minutes, maybe more. Up and down jostles to my hose are carried out. He causes me to breathe incessantly, windswept and dizzy against him. His right hand moves fluently on my pole and sends a vibration of pure bliss throughout my entire system.

Thank God for the closet's frame or I will helplessly fall to the wooden floor and twist an ankle or smash a kneecap. My right fist grips wood as … Jamar grips the wood between my legs. I howl with ecstasy as his fist and fingers react with the extension of meat that sweats and pulsates between my thighs. Chaos is discovered as I whisper the Frenchman's name again and again.

"Cream," Jamar breathes into my ear. "Cream now, Just. Do it for me."

I listen. What else am I supposed to do? Another jolt of pleasure twists and turns within my core. Another howl escapes my lips. Another handy jack occurs to my post and … white fluid erupts from my eight-inch man-lever and twirls into the closet. Sticky cream decorates toilet paper rolls, a new stick of deodorant, hand towels, and unopened shampoo bottles. Endless amounts of the goo sputters out of my tool, glazing a Sensor razor, bars of unopened soap, and a bag of cotton balls. I am emptied with such ease, manipulated by the photographer's palm and fingers, brought to this moment of rich pleasure and sultry desire, now spent and weak, and semi-conscious in front him.

Before he pulls away from me and vanishes inside the bathroom to wash his hands, removing my sticky sap from his appendages, he leans into my ear yet again, and finalizes our connection with one last whisper, "Made you cream. Exactly what I wanted."

2 – PLAYING HARD TO GET

I tell Lincoln about my sexcapade with Jamar in my apartment's hallway, but he doesn't believe me. The cocoa-colored bitch with amethyst-colored eyes says to me with attitude, "Jamar is straight. He dates a blonde woman that works at the Louvre. They're talking about getting married."

I take a sip of my vodka tonic, swallow it down, and admit, "Trust me, I know what happened. The guy couldn't wait to get me off. He had a plan and carried it out."

Lincoln checks out a pack of suave and deliciously dark boys that enter Club Maxine, a local jazz bar we frequent. All of them look fresh out of high school and ready for college. The scholars wear expensive threads and smoke cigars. The pack finds a table near the stage, order drinks from Lucille, one of the club's prized servers, so very ready to take in the next act, a local jazz band called Black Mellon.

My best friend says, "You're barking up the wrong tree, guy. Jamar likes the ladies. In fact, his promiscuous behavior is always landing him in trouble."

"Does he do guys on the side?" I inquire, enjoying the sound of Black Mellon, my beverage, and Lincoln's company.

"Who knows? French men are always ready to jump in the sack. Having an affair in France is accepted in a relationship over there."

"I'm a fling for him. Something different. An American black man at his beck and call."

"Not if you play hard to get," Lincoln suggests.

"That's my problem. I've never played hard to get."

"Of course you haven't. A string of basketball players in this city highly recommend your ass for some man-play," he jokes, always the comedian.

I sort of chuckle, knowing that this information is true. What can I say? I have a thing for basketball players ... and French photographers. "Only the best fuck me."

Lincoln smiles at my statement and shares, "There's a lot of best out there according to that fact."

My beverage is now dry. I point to it on the table, listen to Black Mellon play, and reply, "Fuck you, Lincoln. For that comment, you owe me a drink."

"All your drinks," he confesses, "because you're my dearest friend, and because you're doing me a favor by taking Jamar in for a week."

I become sloppy drunk at the jazz club. So drunk that Lincoln takes me home and makes sure I end up inside my own bed. Once here, he undresses me and puts me to bed. Before leaving, I think he says something like: "I'll check up on you tomorrow."

Under a summer sheet, I close my eyes, drift into a chocolate-colored world with handsome basketball players and a single photographer. Some of the men are naked. Others only wear Unico briefs. The dream I have is quite naughty: a number of sexy black men do a train on my bottom, one after the next, after the next, after the next ...

Does a smile form on my face while I dream? I think so. Do I obtain a firm rod between my legs? I do.

How long do I sleep (an hour ... two hours ... three hours ... four hours) until I mysteriously, but contently, end up in bed with Jamar Louis.

# # # # #

Dawn reaches into my eyes and attempts to smother my brain. I wake in Jamar's naked arms and listen to him ask in his thick French, "Justice, were you lonely last night?"

Both of us have piss boners the size of the Empire State building. And both of us cling together with morning perspiration, a thick aroma of male musk, and bad breath. I reply with: "I don't know how I got here," and confess to drinks with Lincoln at Club Maxine, details regarding the pack of college guys who entered the club, and how Lincoln drove me home for the night, tucking me into bed.

Perhaps, following Lincoln's tucking-me-in ceremony, I drifted into a deep sleep, semi-woke at some early hour when it was still dark outside, discovered the spare bedroom and the Frenchman in his bed. Perhaps I found my way against his dark skin, spooning his muscular body throughout the night. Perhaps I …

Beside me, Jamar inquires, "Are you lovers with Lincoln?"

"Hell no," I burst. "Never would that work out. The two of us are total opposites. We're only friends, and want to remain this way until we both die."

I can always sense when a man wants to become sexually frisky during my company; this is what I perceive about the photographer aligned with my naked skin. These men tell stories of seduction within the corners of their alluring eyes. They tend to hypnotize their male victims and obtain exactly what they want from them. These men – like Jamar now – become predators for sexual attention and want a nipple pinched, the cords that line their muscular necks licked, their pumped abs fingered, and their swollen cocks sucked until they churn their loads. Frenchmen who resemble Jamar want nothing less than to get their rocks off, explode semen against another man's flesh, splattering the goo on their bedmates' faces, wavy tummies, or in their tight-throated mouths. These men are radicals in the bedroom, among other sexual places, and become hungry for nothing but sin because of their sexual longings.

"You have morning wood," Jamar whispers into my left ear as he wraps one of his palms around the pounder between my nicely sculpted thighs.

I push his hand away, playing hard to get; exactly what Lincoln recommends I carry out.

To no avail, my temporary roommate has other things in mind instead of keeping his distance from me. With one hand-swoop, the summer sheet is removed from my body and exposes the eight inches of timber-hard shaft lying flat against my stomach. Again, his hand finds the upright dong at my middle, leashing fingers around its plumpness. A quick and heated stroke ensues ... two strokes ... three strokes, and I gasp with unequivocal pleasure on the bed, dizzy, helpless, and so very much under his expected spell. My hips jut upward, into his fist, and another gasp of excitement exits my semi-parted lips. Within seconds, a bubble of ooze leaks out of my tool, onto his fingers and knuckles and ...

If I don't pull away from his closeness, I will inevitably blow my load. If I don't play hard to get, I will surely surrender to his man-connected-man touch and willfully continue to buck my hips into his fist until I burst with oozy pleasure. If I don't become easy with the dark-skinned Frenchman, he will crave my skin even more.

The decision is made rather spontaneously to push his hand away for the second time. What follows is nothing less than a hurried action of my body leaping off the bed. In the process, my upright shaft swings to the left and right, teasing the young photographer as if it has magical powers to connect men in bliss.

"Come back here," he demands, patting the empty spot next to him on the bed. "Don't be running away like that."

He's beautiful on the bed. No, he's ... stunning. His eyes seem to light up the room in the morning's dim, golden-rays. The man's lips are ever so slightly spread apart and look plump, utterly kissable. Bubbles of perspiration dapple his brown shoulders. His nipples gleam a shiny cocoa hue on their mounded pecs. Jamar's lined stomach is flat and delicious looking. The ten inches of veined and uncut pole between his striking legs look irresistible and cause me to lick my lips. I study its solid mass and accessorizing balls that are clean-shaven and quite smooth. Again, I lick my lips; this time out of pure hunger, need, and an unbelievable attraction.

Jamar sees the infatuation on my face for his body and reaches for the cement cock between his legs. Two fingers wrap around its head and he pulls it away from his torso, releases the tube of meat, and it snaps against his rigid abdominals. In doing so, he chants in French, "*Me donner un tour.*"

I translate his French rather accurately this time: "Give me a ride."

"Now," he utters in English, and snaps his cock a second time. Pre-juice twirls out of its mushroom-capped head and nails one of his nipples.

Walk away, Justice. Go while you can. Play hard to get. Lincoln whispers between my temples, assisting my thoughts.

"I won't," I utter, and bite my bottom lip. Within seconds, I head to the spare bedroom's door and begin my exit.

"Justice," he chants from the bed. "Justice, I … like you."

I keep walking and close the door behind me. Now, I head to my own bedroom, locking myself inside. And here, I toy with the spike between my thighs until I fire off a load, decorating my stomach, pecs, and my chin.

3 – THE COLOR OF LUST

"Jamar's cock was hard to turn away from," I admit to Lincoln. "There's no way he's straight."

"I don't see how either statement is possible," he says, admitting to me that Jamar's photography shoot was the best he has ever seen and calls the man sexy as hell, robust, and a black god behind his professional Minoltas, Nikons, and Canons. "If I didn't have Shane, I would drop my pants for Jamar, and he could fuck me any way he wanted."

I laugh at this, admiring my friend's honesty. This time, we are at a bear bar called Business: Black. The place is sleek and rather masculine with black and grey steel bar stools, expensive sofas, and matching tables. The platinum-colored stage is empty tonight, seeming lifeless without a blues singer or pianist. Instead, creamy brown or dark chocolate-hued men in suits with big muscles and inflated egos frequent the place this evening. Think closeted, black Wall Street. Think high-powered executives of color who like to ram dicks into coffee-colored, eighteen-year-old boys. Think black weathermen, bankers, professors, insurance salesman, politicians, city realtors, and advertising agents. It's the perfect place to gain a husband; someone who is of an oak brown hue with a large slammer between his high-powered legs and a matching wallet.

"To the color of lust," I raise my vodka tonic and make a toast with him.

"Cheers," Lincoln adds, grinning from ear to ear.

We drink in silence, watching white-collared men hit on pretty black boys, willing to take one or two home, or back to their executive offices for a night's fling, tossing them away tomorrow morning.

Following our toast, Lincoln asks, "Will you ever settle down?"

"Eventually. I just haven't met the right man yet."

"Are you still doing the online dating gig?"

I shake my head, take a sip of my strong drink, swallow, and confess, "I gave that up three weeks ago."

Now, he surprises me and asks, "Could Jamar be the right guy for you?"

I place my drink on the bar, gain all of his attention with my questioning stare, and prattle, "First you want me to play hard to get, and now you want me to marry him."

He laughs at me: humbly, warmly, without insult. He shakes his head and explains, "I'm not saying that at all. You always have to leave your options open, though, right?"

I get him; I have always understood him. "Jamar is hot. Sexy as a motherfucker and about as rock-hard handsome as a model. I think we get along just fine."

"No problems with him staying at your apartment then, right?"

"None. Half the time, I don't even know he's there."

Lincoln clears his throat, ignoring the cell call from his lover, Shane, for the time being. He reaches out and grabs my right kneecap, startling me. In doing so, he challenges, "I think you should try him out for size before he heads back to Paris."

"What do you mean by 'for size'?" I inquire.

"You know … his attraction for you. See what he's like in bed."

"This is completely opposite of what you told me earlier. You said he was straight."

My friend laughs and confesses with a broad smile, "You're right. I know. I'm just saying that … some guys will stray from their straight pathways and fall for a cock or two, and then a guy's heart. If the sex is good, they'll come back for more. Then they won't leave."

"Techniques of nailing a black man."

I make him laugh: white teeth, tiny wrinkles around his amethyst-colored eyes, slightly raised ears. "Try him out for size, Just. If he doesn't like you … or you don't like him after the week is over … he returns to France and you get your life back. Who knows what can happen from this arrangement."

"You're horrible for advice, man, and confusing," I claim.

"I know," he admits, and drinks way too much in the next two hours, which forces me to drive him home.

4 – RAW JUSTICE

It's almost one o'clock in the morning when I find my way back to my apartment. I climb the stairs, try not to jingle keys at its front door, enter quietly, and make my way to my bedroom in the dark. Once inside my bedroom, streetlight spills into the confines and … Jamar is a mere shadow of naked beauty on my bed's surface. Again, he is rock-hard, and ready for a ride. But, he lightly snores, under a dream's spell, and flat on his back with his arms spread wide.

I peel off my clothes, dropping them to the bedroom floor. I now head to the bathroom to brush my teeth and wash my face. Within minutes, I return to my bedroom and the Frenchman in my bed. Carefully, I manage to climb in bed, snuggle against his ash-scented skin, and drift off to sleep.

The clinging of one man to another man transpires at some point during the night: a mix of a coffee shop owner and photographer underneath the soothing and tranquil beauty of city street lights. What transpires between us is nothing less than poetic bliss, a blending of an American and Frenchman on a queen-sized Sealy Posturepedic mattress. Our dark skin collides rather easily, and we begin to perform naughty XXX movements together; the queer dance of two black men.

"Jamar," floats out of my plump lips as the temporary guest climbs between my spread legs and devours my erection with his hungry throat. Sexual chaos is discovered as four of my eight inches delve into his tight and wet system. A gasp of pure elation exits my mouth, which fills the bedroom. My palms collide with the back of the photographer's head. Fingertips dig into his scalp. And I instruct rather briskly, "Take it all, man. Devour every last inch."

The Frenchman listens. His head bobs up and down on my tool. Inch after pulsating inch of my black beef blocks his throat as he blows me. He loses oxygen, gags a few times on my veined rod, but doesn't seem to stop his north and south suction, obviously pleased with his mouthy work.

Of course I can pop my creamy and sticky load into his face-cavern, but the foreigner decides to pull off and away from my ooze-spigot in a brisk motion, having other XXX ideas in mind.

To my utter surprise, under the photographer's sexual care, my ass is lifted by his massive palms, and I lock my feet behind my head. The man uses his fingertips to pry my bottom open for his use. During this early morning hour, he bows his beautiful, model-like face to my puckered ass and licks the tight opening with satisfied groans. These nighttime licks turn into steadfast laps, though, one after the next, which send me into a state of pulsing joy, caught under his touch.

"Jamar," exits my mouth yet again, but I am not heard. The man is on a sexual mission to pleasure us both. One of his zealous laps to my core turn into dozens as he attempts to satisfy his black-ass hunger to its fullest. Again and again, the guy eats my back passage, into his gig, a selfish game that can elementarily be called Raw Justice.

With certainty, I am prepared to wash my chocolate-colored torso down with self-spew. My act does not occur at this very minute, though. Instead, the photographer pulls his face away from my ripe behind, spanks its guy-slit with three fingers, and announces with a lift in his masculine voice, "It's cock-time, Justice. I hope you're ready."

# # # # #

With a condom affixed to his French sword, he lifts my bottom up, connects my feet to the back of my head again, and stands above me on the bed's mattress, directing his tool at my black hole. Here, he pushes one, plastic-coated inch into my constricted chasm, separating my ass cheeks with his smooth palms, keeping them locked to my skin to balance himself. The inch pulls out and two inches push inside, readying my rump for the rest of his spike's massive length. Now, the two inches rise out of my man-cave and three ... four ... five ... six inches are shoved inside.

A gasp and grunt escape my lungs. I shiver beneath him and feel tears surface at the corners of my eyes. I reply with a whimper, "All of it, man … Put it all inside me."

The only response by Jamar is simple: he slides the six inches of meat out of my middle and slams all ten inside me with immediate friction.

Pain rocks every organ inside my torso. My heartbeat races and perspiration lines my forehead, shoulders, chest, and legs. Every pore along my body's flesh puddles with sweat. I rock up and down on the mattress as he stands above me, banging my bottom. The bed squeaks under our devised motion.

How long does he ride me while standing on the bed, directing his shaft inside my narrow and tight crevice? Do ten minutes turn into seventeen minutes with utter simplicity? Does his ten-inch rod really stay hard for this length of time, pushing into my central hub, pulling out with speed, and pushing in yet again … again … again?

I become a black man-toy beneath him. His American pet. The coffee shop owner turns into a Frenchman's game. My rear is banged continuously, dramatically, without a single break. I moan, grunt, growl, and murmur beneath his power-driving motion.

Jamar utters something in French that I can't understand. Repeatedly, he plunges his bolt into my guy-canal. With uncontrolled power, he rises and falls while still standing on the mattress, and pulverizes my bulbous posterior.

"Coming," surfaces from my mouth without notice. Truth is I blow my load without even having my cock touched. A shiver rushes through my chest and burns between my temples with deep satisfaction. My balls become fiery orbs between my legs, producing a rush of white spray. Every ab on my stomach tingles with pure delight. Having no control of my orgasm whatsoever, sticky seed rushes out of my pole and splashes against my chest, inside my mouth, and decorates my chin.

Three, heavy grunts roll out of Jamar's chest as he rocks up and down, inside my man-end. Sweat flies against my ass. With a final tug, removing his meaty apparatus from its cozy lust-place, he tells me in French that he is ready to blow.

His burst-gig occurs rather quickly. The Frenchman jacks his ten-inch post with both fists. One … two … three immediate tugs happen with utter brilliance, a handy build-up to what is about to transpire between us.

On my back now, perpendicular to his standing body, I stare up at his chiseled frame in a state of hungry likeness. Within seconds, following the guest's north and south motion on his dick, I am sprinkled, splashed, and sprayed with his French load. Foreign goo fills the indentation of my chocolaty navel. The cream lines all of my sweaty and muscular abs. Ooze garnishes my nipples, neck, and chin as the black god above me fully drains his hose.

His look says he is spent: sunken eyes, cherry red face, sweat lathering his chest. It's a look of happiness mixed with complete exhaustion, which he seems to wear very well.

# # # # #

Afterward, out of breath and stingingly spent, Jamar falls to the bed. During this period of my cottony clean-up with a bath towel, I watch the man's bulky chest rise and fall. Here and now, in the folds of an American night in New York City, very much at my side, the post-sexed foreigner whispers something to me in his beautiful and elegant language that I only somewhat can translate; a phrase or string of words that is beyond my Level II French skills in his romantic speak.

"Translate," I say, curious of what he has just shared with me.

"I want to stay with you, if you will have me, Just."

Overwhelmed by his confession, glowing within my bedroom like a summer garden insect that flickers on/off … on/off … on/off … I lean my lips against his left cheek, and provide his sexy skin with a city boy's American kiss.

"Very nice," he admits, delighted with my company. "I stay until you don't like me."

My left palm rolls down and over his sculpted, black chest that I find sexy-hot and comfortable with my touch. Fingers study his mounded abs once again and travel southward bound, where they wrap around his still-firm, ten inches of lust. Here, I squeeze leftover sap out its capped head, just for my own personal amusement and deep satisfaction. And here, at his side, two black guys from different countries and backgrounds who have discovered an emotional connection with our hearts and naked skin, I reply rather endearingly, and honestly, to his comment with: "Stay as long as you would like. I'm sure I won't become bored with you and your black goods anytime soon."

CATTLE DRIVE
By Jay Starre

Residing on English Bay in Vancouver, Canada, Jay Starre has pumped out steamy gay fiction for dozens of anthologies and has written two gay erotic novels. Contact Jay Starre on Facebook

RJ tied his horse to the slender trunk of a willow and crept down the deer trail between alder and birch to finally settle on his belly behind the broad trunk of an oak. From here, he could spy unseen on the Pecos River below.

He wasn't stalking animals or even Indians. He wasn't on the look-out for stray cattle from the herd they pushed north toward Wyoming. No. He was spying on Lincoln, his fellow cowboy about to strip down and take a bath in the cool river water.

The sun was low in the west and the heat of the day abating, especially with the cool air hovering above the stream. He was still sweating, though, and even more now as he was rewarded for his stealthy journey down the path by the thrilling sight of his buddy getting naked.

"Oh god dammit and bless me if I'm not going straight to hell," he whispered, clutching the stiffening bone under his trail-dusty trousers.

Lincoln was really tall and all ropy muscle. His skin glinted like polished ebony in the hazy afternoon sunlight. Once his cowboy hat was tossed aside, the close-cropped curls of his black hair formed a perfect cap around his skull. His bold features were emphasized by regular shaving, more regular than most of the other cowboys they wrangled with.

His tooled burgundy boots, made special by a Hispano down in Tucson, ended up beside his hat, shirt and kerchief. Next, off came his pants. RJ peered around the bole of the oak, breathless as he squeezed the bulge in his own trousers and bit back gasps of appreciation.

His ass, black as the rest of him, jutted out from a slim waist in twin globes of solid power. His broad back and long limbs were hairless and utterly smooth. With his back to RJ, he picked his way through the dry grass down to the water and dove in.

When he came back up, he let out a whoop and turned to face the slope. He used the bar of soap he'd clutched in his hand when he dove in and began scrubbing away the grime of the trail, from head to toe.

The cowboy behind the oak tree watched the show with wide-eyed fascination. He got a good look at the lengthy pole dangling down between his buddy's thighs and couldn't resist pulling his own out to start pumping it. He'd caught tantalizing glimpses of the black snake a number of times along the trail, but he could never get enough of the sight of it. Many a night he fell asleep beside the fire fantasizing about that long black rod.

They'd been riding together on the Skimmerhorn Trail for weeks now, and would ride for weeks more before they delivered the thousand longhorns destined for the trail head up north. The two had become buddies right away, even though they were as different as night and day.

Lincoln was a black from Tennessee and the son of slaves, while RJ was a red-headed Yankee out of Boston spawned from Irish immigrants. Lincoln was smart as a whip and RJ was so quiet most everyone considered him a simpleton, though he wasn't.

The black was popular with the other cowboys, mostly because he could both read and write. It had been against the law in the Old South for slaves to learn to do either before the Civil War, and so after emancipation Lincoln's father insisted his brood of free-born children learn what he'd been forbidden.

He wrote letters for the other cowboys and even read to them around the campfire in the evenings from the books he'd brought along. He did all the letter writing and ledger keeping for the Trail Boss, too. He spoke elegantly and hardly ever cursed. And he was a damn good cowboy.

RJ idolized him. To his utter consternation, the tall cowboy had taken him under his wing from the first day. Like a puppy dog, he followed Lincoln everywhere, and the lanky cowboy didn't seem to mind.

Today, he'd followed as usual, but at a discrete distance and without Lincoln's knowledge.

Lincoln rinsed off and strode up out of the water, naked as the day he was born. RJ shuddered and emitted a little moan as his active imagination ran riot. What he would love to do with that handsome cowboy! The range of nasty positions he dreamed of seemed endless in scope. But he was far too timid to even hint at anything like that to his friend.

The tall cowboy went to his palomino gelding, Teaser, and unlaced his rolled-up blanket then brought it over to a soft spot in the high grass just above the river bank. Still naked, he sprawled out on the blanket with his rolled-up clothes for a pillow.

He began to stroke his cock!

RJ's bright blue eyes nearly bulged out of his head as he rose up onto his knees for a better look – and for better access to his own stiff cock. That movement, and the slight shift in the breeze, alerted Teaser to his presence. The gelding tossed his head and whinnied.

The horse loved RJ, as did all the other horses. He treated them with a gentle tenderness that many of the other cowboys just didn't have in them. Teaser had smelled him and now called out to him.

"Come on down here, RJ. Get your rear end in the river and wash up. The herd will be grazing for the next few hours, so we got a spell to idle away before we got to get back."

He'd been caught out! Lincoln hadn't even glanced his way, but with unerring instinct knew whom his horse called out to. There was nothing for RJ to do but make his way down to join him.

He quickly stuffed his stiff cock back in his trousers, then pink-faced and mumbling an apology, he arrived to stand in front of Lincoln. He was unable to tear his eyes from the cowboy's black cock and the hand that still pumped it idly. Coated in glistening spit, it was a semi-stiff tower rearing up from his crotch and growing bigger by the moment!

"The soap's on that rock there. Get naked, cowboy, and get scrubbed up. This big old black dick will still be here when you get back."

RJ's bright blue eyes gleamed, contrasting with the freckled complexion that now blazed pink. "Sure, Lincoln. Sure thing," he blurted out.

Just hearing his buddy say something nasty like that had him shaking from head to toe. Lincoln did not go on about women and sex like the other cowboys often did. To hear him talk about his dick, while pumping it right in front of him, was shocking – and so exciting he could barely stand it.

Little did he realize how much filthier the smiling cowboy's language was about to get – along with his actions!

With trembling hands, he undid the buttons of his trousers and pushed them down to his ankles, his underwear along with them. He stripped in a rush of mingled fear and excitement. His own boner betrayed his true feelings, naturally, and with those large dark eyes watching his every move, he felt more exposed than ever before in his young life.

Lincoln's rumbling chuckle thrilled him, while eliciting another wave of shivers up and down his body. He tried not to think about his stiff cock waving in front of him and his bare butt wagging behind him as he trotted bare foot down to the river bank and snatched up the soap Lincoln had left there.

That bath was like no other he'd ever taken. Acutely aware of his buddy above watching his every move, he ran the soap over his muscular chest and broad shoulders then down to his smooth belly and over his jutting dick. Looking up at Lincoln, he rubbed the soapy froth into the pink pole self-consciously but couldn't help pumping for a moment or two as the cowboy above nodded and grinned, rubbing his own black pole with languid strokes.

"Turn around and show me that white butt while you scrub it, RJ."

Standing in the cool water half-way up his calves, he picked his way over the stones beneath his feet and turned around as directed. He felt Lincoln's eyes boring into him as he reached back and began to soap up his hefty butt-cheeks.

He was short and stocky with an especially powerful lower body. His thighs were slightly bowed from riding since he was just a kid, but were thick with muscle. Even his calves bulged. His ass was huge, utterly pale and smooth, with a deep divide between the full mounds. It made for a great cushion in the saddle, but at the moment all he could think of was that big black cock and how Lincoln stroked it – while watching him soap up his butt.

Timid by nature, those lurid thoughts were probably the reason behind his next actions, which were totally out of character for him. He found himself bending over at the waist as his soapy fingers slipped into his own deep butt valley and began lathering it up. He even spread his feet wider apart so that the crack opened up.

Gasping at his own temerity, he couldn't help himself and got even nastier. A soapy finger settled on his pink asshole and then as if under someone else's control, slithered up into his gut.

He was fingering himself!

His finger slid in and out of his asshole along with a froth of soapy bubbles. He grunted aloud at the sensual ache, unable to prevent the nasty thoughts that bombarded him from growing even more specific. Instead of that slender pink finger, he imagined Lincoln's lengthy black dick sliding in and out. He crammed his finger in one more time, even deeper, before Lincoln's rumbling voice interrupted.

"Now that is something I find downright titillating, cowboy. Rinse off and get on up here, so I can inspect that butt a might bit closer."

Again, he obeyed without question. Straightening up and pulling his finger from his own asshole, he flushed from head-to-toe as he realized what he'd just been doing, and what Lincoln must think of him.

Yet at the same time, he was seized by a thrilling sense of liberation. He trusted the tall cowboy, with his life, and there was no reason to let shyness keep him from doing what he wanted most.

With that determination bolstering his stride, he did his best not to be embarrassed as he came back up the slope with pink boner bobbing in front of him. The big grin that Lincoln offered while he slowly pumped a hand up and down his own stiff cock encouraged him, but also gave him pause. If he was lucky enough to be offered it, how would he ever get all that cock up his butt?

His look of fearful interest was clear and Lincoln laughed out loud. "Kneel down here between my legs. Let's see that sweet smile of yours, cowboy. Let's see those pretty pink lips of yours open wide and suck in this big cowboy cock. You know you want to."

"Yep, sure, sure I want to, Lincoln," he managed to spit out as he dropped to his knees on the blanket between those long black thighs and did as he was told.

The boner reared up in front of him. Midnight-black and coated with Lincoln's frothy spit, it twitched in his hand, a sign of how much it wanted his lips around it. With a gulp and a nervous grin, he lowered his face and opened wide.

His lips, bowed and pink, found the bullet-shaped head. He groaned aloud as he took it in.

Lincoln encouraged him with a stream of nasty talk.

Marcus Anthony

"Get your mouth over that cock, Boy. Suck it. Yeah, just like that. Get your ass over here, too, so I can feel it. Now that's a fine cowboy ass. Spread your legs, RJ. Open that ass up. You like that? You like my fingers running around in that deep crack? You like my fingers tickling your cowboy asshole? Come on, wriggle that fine cowboy ass for me. Show me how much you like it. Do you like it enough to let me put my big cowboy cock up inside it? I bet you do; I bet you do."

He kept up that spew of filthy encouragement as RJ felt himself growing hot all over and burning up with nasty need. Everything the tall cowboy said was true! He wanted to suck that black cock, to wrap his lips around it, to taste it, to suck it deep. He wanted that huge snake up his tender, hungry ass, too! He wanted it so bad he thought he might actually die if he didn't get it.

He'd crawled around so that he knelt beside Lincoln's chest with his bare butt handy for the cowboy to fondle, while still sucking that beautiful black cock with loud slurps and smacks. Now that he had it in his mouth, he just couldn't get enough of it.

But the hands on his butt were driving him crazy, too! Lincoln had big hands, and although they were calloused like all cowboys from holding the reins and roping and branding and such, he kept them clean and used liberal amounts of creamy ointment to keep them from cracking and peeling. The fingertips slid over the wide expanse of his hairless white butt in a satiny glide, then trailed up and down his parted crack with teasing strokes that had him wriggling and heaving that large can enthusiastically.

Lincoln's dirty talk got him even more worked up. "That's it, cowboy, rub that white butt against my fingertips. I got to say, RJ, your butt is downright vo-lup-tuous. Yep, downright vo-lup-tuous." He spoke each syllable with emphasis, a mannerism of his when reading aloud to the cowboys in the evenings, especially with words they would find unfamiliar.

He went on. "My fingers love that ass and that crack, and you like them, too, I know you do. Come on; get deeper down on that black cock. Open up your throat, you know you want to. Yeah, boy, just like

145

that. Rub that big butt against my fingers while you gargle with my stiff black dick. Would you like me to lick that ass of yours? Want me to tickle this tender little hole with my tongue? I bet you do. I bet you do."

RJ drooled and gurgled as he attempted the nearly impossible, driving down over that lengthy pole to get it all the way in. His experience at cock-sucking was limited, but he was so excited it seemed like he might even be able to do it! Listening to Lincoln's deep voice spewing out that thrilling dirty talk only helped.

Lincoln's actions followed on the heels of his nasty words. He lifted RJ's leg up and over his chest so that he was now kneeling with his ass in the black cowboy's face. Suddenly feeling a tongue dive up into his spread crack, he grunted with exhilarated determination and opened wide enough to allow the tapered crown to slither past his tonsils and deep into his throat.

As he found his lips actually sliding to the base of that lengthy cock, a tongue attacked his puckered asshole and began to worm its way into him. He jerked wildly over Lincoln's warm dark body as he felt himself invaded from both ends at once.

Broad dark hands gripped his pale butt-cheeks and spread them wide. Tongue jabbed into him. Silky lips clamped over his hole and massaged it. He felt split in two, his ass wide open and his ass-lips quivering apart with a will of their own. That tongue dove deeper, and deeper.

He felt all that cock throbbing in his throat and found himself again imagining it doing the same thing up inside his tender asshole. He moaned and squirmed as he began to bob up and down over Lincoln's cock, letting it slide in and out of his throat with surprising ease.

The black cowboy pulled off RJ's hole just long enough to encourage him with more lurid talk. "Suck that cock, cowboy! Get it deep in your throat so that my black balls are banging against your chin. You like all that hot meat in your mouth, don't you? You like wrapping your pretty lips around that stiff black bone. I know you do, boy. Want that tongue back up your ass, too? Wriggle your big white butt if you do, yeah, like that. Yeah, you know you want me to tongue-fuck that snug little hole of yours before I fuck it. You know you do."

He crammed his face back into RJ's parted crack and attacked his pink hole again. His slurps galvanized the young cowboy to even more efforts at sucking his hot cock. He swallowed it to the root and held it there until he ran out of breath, then pulled all the way off with a gasp, then did the same thing again. And again.

The tongue and lips assaulting his tender hole had him feeling all wet and loose back there, and believing it might be possible to take all of Lincoln's cock up his butt. Already, from how Lincoln had been acting so far, he knew that once the black cowboy got his cock up there, he wasn't going to take no for an answer. He'd plow RJ good and hard and good and deep!

Lincoln was thinking along the same lines, but had his own method in mind of going about it. Again, he pulled his face out of RJ's deep crack and gave his nasty orders.

"Before I fill this vo-lup-tuous ass of yours with cock, you got to show me how much you want it. Ride my tongue, RJ. Ride it like you're going to ride my cock. You know you want to."

He crammed his face back in RJ's deep crack and his tongue back in the pink hole. The red-head groaned around the cock in his throat as he began to vigorously follow his buddy's instructions. He humped the tongue burrowing into his tender hole with rearing hips, slamming down onto the broad nose and wide mouth in his crack while he continued to bob over the lengthy cock in his mouth.

He couldn't believe how that felt. He was stuffed from both ends. His knees were splayed wide, his ass open and his hole gaping for the tongue sliding in and out of it. His mouth gaped, too, and black cock rode in and out of it. The warm, solid body under his felt amazing, while those large black hands gripped his melon-cheeks fiercely as they rose and fell and rose and fell.

He could have gone on forever like that, but Lincoln was calling the shots. He decided it was time to move on.

His tongue came out of that quivering slot and his lips smacked lewdly as he gave his orders. "Get your rear end off my face and get on over to Teaser and fetch my ointment from my saddle bags. Time to apply a liberal coating of something slippery in that deep butt crack of yours. You know what for, RJ, don't you? Tell me why we got to slippery-up that crack of yours."

The red-head was rising as he answered, his legs rubbery and breathless from all that enthusiastic cock-sucking. But he was able to answer, surprising himself at his ability to speak so freely.

"We got to grease up my big white butt good so's your big black cock can fuck it. That's why we need that ointment, Lincoln. We need it so you can fuck my butt good and hard."

"That's right, cowboy. And you know you want it. You know you do."

He trotted over to Teaser, his pink cock bobbing and drooling and his big white butt-cheeks jiggling. The gelding whinnied and licked his bare shoulder as he searched in the saddle bags for the jar of ointment. He found it and raced back to Lincoln.

The black cowboy had used the brief break to pull the blanket a little higher on the bank, so he could lean against a boulder. He also combined RJ's discarded clothing with his own to create a comfortable backrest. Now he sat nearly upright with his lean thighs sprawled wide and his muscular arms folded behind his neck. His cock reared up from his lap, an ink-black column of rigid heat. RJ shuddered and actually moaned aloud as he contemplated what was about to happen.

"Time for some lu-bri-cation, RJ. Grease up this big cock. You know you want to."

He dropped like a stone between Lincoln's thighs and twisted open the lid of the small glass jar in his hands. The ointment he scooped out was slightly green and smelled like cottonwood. A Navaho squaw had made a good supply of it for Lincoln, and he'd been generous enough to give some to RJ. He knew how good it felt on his hands after a rough day of wrangling, and now he was about to find out how good it would feel on another part of his body, a much more intimate part!

He rubbed the paste over Lincoln's cock, feeling it melt immediately into a silken coating that glistened brightly over the onyx-dark flesh. Somehow, it made the lengthy pole look even more exciting now that it gleamed so brutally black in the soft early-evening light.

"Turn around and squat over my lap, RJ. I want to see that plump white butt of yours while you ride my cock. And give me that ointment so I can rub some of it into your crack."

The red-head obeyed, more than content to let Lincoln be the boss. He turned and straddled his hips, then squatted down over his lap. He felt that black cock ride up between his parted butt-cheeks, a rigid pole of slippery heat. He reached back to hand off the jar of ointment then a moment later felt fingers probing into his spread crack beside that lengthy cock.

They stroked up and down, coating the deep valley with the slippery goo. RJ leaned forward and placed his hands on the blanket between Lincoln's dark thighs, lifting his ass so that those fingers had total access to his crack.

They ran over his hole, and he let out a gasp then they settled on it and rubbed all over it. Fingertips added more ointment. And more. A pair of them began to gently push at the puckered entrance. He moaned and wriggled his ass against them.

"Yep, cowboy. Downright vo-lup-tuous, that is one fine ass. You want my fingers up that fine butt, RJ? You want me to dig them into your tender little hole? Do you?"

"Yes! Yes I do! Please put your big black fingers up my white butt, Lincoln!"

Lincoln's rumbling chuckle was followed by a pressure against the red-head's quivering sphincter, then a slithering glide as two greased fingers invaded his aching gut. He cried out but didn't attempt to escape the powerful pressure. He did the opposite. He sat down on those fingers and managed to swallow them up, right past the second knuckle.

"Good boy, very good boy! You like that, you know you do. Just imagine how much you'll like my cock up there! Just imagine it, cowboy. Imagine this stiff piece of hot meat sliding way up this tender hole of yours."

As he talked, he pumped his fingers deeper, twisted them, and then pulled them back out, stretching the rim as he did. RJ grunted and wriggled wildly, arching his back and squatting deeper. That allowed his ass-lips to gape wider open. Lincoln laughed aloud as he took full advantage of the opportunity to probe deeper.

He slowly stuffed his fingers back inside, turning and twisting as he did. He massaged the tender lips with his knuckles and then buried them as far as he could before slowly pulling them back out.

"You like that, cowboy, don't you? Don't you? Tell me how much you like it. Don't be fas-tidious, tell me how much you like me rooting around in this hungry hole of yours."

RJ answered between grunts of pleasure. "Yes ... uuhhnnngg ... yes ... yes, Lincoln I like those fingers up my butt! Uhhnnngg ... I love them up my butt!"

The black cowboy laughed some more as he took his time digging around with his slippery fingers, enjoying the sight of his dark digits thrusting into the bright pink hole. He yanked them out, then jabbed them deep a few more times before he replaced them with the head of his cock.

"Time for you to ride some cowboy cock. Go ahead, sit down on it. You know you want to. You know you want to so bad, don't you, RJ?"

"Yessir, Lincoln! I want it so bad, so goddamn bad!"

He pushed back against the slippery cock-head and was rewarded by the sensation of heated flesh slithering past his well-greased butt rim. It went in with remarkable ease, and not only because both hole and cock were liberally coated with ointment. In that position, squatting over Lincoln's lap, his ass and hole were wide open. And it helped that the cowboy's dark dick had a slim head.

Still, there was an awful lot of cock below that tapered crown!

"Go on, squat deep, you know you want it, cowboy."

He dropped lower, gasping as more cock slid up into him. And more. It felt amazing inside him, filling him with rigid, throbbing heat. He wanted even more! He began to hump it, rising and falling, lowering himself farther with every heave of his white butt.

"Show me how much you want that big black cock. That's it, cowboy. Ride it. Sit right down on it."

"Yessir! Oh ... oh ... oh ... yessir!"

He couldn't believe how it felt as he got more and more of it deeper into his gut. Every time he drove downwards, he felt the slippery head find another aching spot deeper inside him. That sensation fed on itself. He lunged down toward Lincoln's lap. He was almost there!

"Downright vo-lup-tous, downright vol-up-tuous," Lincoln remarked in his deep rumble as he gripped both full ass-cheeks with his dark hands and squeezed them.

That proved enough for RJ to succeed in his heaving assault on Lincoln's long pole. He slammed his fleshy butt against the cowboy's lap, swallowing cock to the root.

They both shouted, startling Teaser, before Lincoln abruptly altered their positions. He relinquished his grip on RJ's round ass-cheeks and moved his arms upward to wrap them around the stocky cowboy's chest. He pulled him backwards and against his own lean torso.

"I am going to fuck this fine, vo-lup-tuous cowboy ass, RJ. And you are going to like it. Aren't you? Aren't you?"

"Yessir! I am going to like your goddamn big black cock fucking my goddamn big white ass," he shouted back, no longer afraid to voice his emotions, now that cock was buried in his gut and it felt so amazing.

Those powerful arms held him in place as Lincoln began to thrust upwards into his greased asshole. The slippery ointment squished around the black pole as it drove upwards and oozed from the violated pink hole as it gulped and swallowed.

Now RJ experienced some entirely new sensations. Not only was he full of rigid cock, he was getting massaged relentlessly by the slamming head and pumping shank. His hole felt like it was on fire!

He leaned back and reveled in it. Content to let Lincoln do all the work, he flopped his thighs wide apart and relaxed his asshole, allowing the pumping black cock to pound him without any resistance.

"You like that. I know you do. You like that black dick riding your hungry cowboy hole. You like it! You know you do!"

"I like it, Lincoln! I like it!"

"That's fine, cowboy. But you aren't liking it enough, not near enough. I'll show you how much more you can like it."

RJ wasn't sure what Lincoln meant until he dropped one hand down to his crotch and seized his rearing pink dick. He had forgotten all about his cock. His asshole had been feeling so fine, it seemed all that mattered. But now, the black cowboy was showing him what he was missing.

One hand began to stroke his cock while the other pinched and tugged at his nipples. The two added sensations drove him wild. He began to buck up and down over the cock up his ass, no longer merely allowing it to drive in and out on its own.

Lincoln reached down with his fingers and scooped up some of the ointment oozing from RJ's hole, then used it to coat his pink cock. His hand pumped up and down the thick pole as his long black cock pummeled in and out.

"Oh! Oh! I like it Lincoln! I really like it! Ohhhhhhh!!!"

He looked down at his pale body, sweaty and heaving, one black hand on his pale chest pinching his nipples, another black hand pumping his pink hard-on, and that dark cock pumping up between his splayed white thighs, and he felt as if he had died and gone to heaven. This was better than any of his nasty dreams.

"Show me how much you like it, RJ. Show me! You know what I want!"

He understood, and had no choice but to obey in any case. The pounding of his tender hole along with the pinching of his nipples and pumping of his cock were more than enough to drive him over the edge. He'd believed he was in heaven before, but now he knew for sure he was. His entire body rocked and vibrated with the power of his orgasm. The driving cock up his ass seemed even more intense as cum shot up his own cock and erupted in a violent spew that reached as far as his chin.

"That's it, cowboy. Give me your cum! Shoot a big load all over yourself with my big black cock up your vo-lup-tuous ass!"

Lincoln continued ramming deep until the final drops of jizz dribbled out of RJ's cock, then hardly missing a beat, he rolled them over so the young red-head found himself on his back, cock slipping from his aching hole and suddenly rearing in his face.

"You know what I want, now, don't you, cowboy? You want it, too, I know you do."

Lincoln grinned down at him as he straddled his face, one hand on the base of his rigid cock and the other grasping RJ's chin. He thought the tall cowboy was going to feed him his cock again, but that wasn't what he had in mind.

He scooted forward just enough so that it wasn't his cock in RJ's face, but his hot black ass! Laughing, he sat down on the red-head and began to rub his crack all over the cowboy's flushed and freckled face.

RJ immediately began licking the black divide while he reached up and grabbed hold of the grinding ass-cheeks. They were so solid! Jutting out from a slim waist, they were like twin globes of sable marble. He fondled and stroked them as that ass-crack moved back and forth over his chin, mouth and nose.

He inhaled the musky stench while tasting the sweaty ass. It was wonderful.

"You like that, don't you? You like that black ass in your pink face. Lick it, cowboy! Get that tongue on my black hole. Show me how much you like it!"

He lapped at the hole, amazed at how tight it was. He clamped his lips over it and began to suck earnestly and was rewarded by the snug lips pouting outwards.

"Yep, cowboy! You know what I want! Suck on that black hole! You know you like it!"

Lincoln's deep voice had risen an octave as he pumped his cock and settled down over those sucking lips. He'd stopped grinding back and forth although his knees squeezed tight around RJ's face as he ass sat right down and his hole began to gape open.

The young cowboy stabbed into the yielding hole with his tongue. Lincoln let out a shout then his entire body convulsed as his cock erupted in a splattering arc of spooge.

RJ tongued deeper, which seemed to drive the black cowboy into fits of further ecstasy. His firm ass vibrated in the red-head's hands. His gasps and grunts filled the air. For the moment, he seemed speechless.

That lasted until the black cowboy's dick finally stopped spewing. It seemed like a long time, but RJ wasn't complaining. Now that he'd gotten a taste of that dark hole, he couldn't get enough of it.

The lanky cowboy slid down and off RJ's face though, until they were lying side-by-side on the blanket and gazing into each other's eyes. They shared satisfied smiles and said nothing for a few minutes as the birds chirped in the oak tree above and the stream bubbled rhythmically below.

Eventually, the garrulous black cowboy spoke. His words were music to RJ's ears.

"From the moment we met, I knew we'd get along just fine, RJ. And we do, don't we? Don't we?"

"Just fine, Lincoln. More than just fine!"

A dark hand slid down his back and past his waist. Black fingers slithered into his deep crack. Moaning, he lifted his knee and thigh to open it up as those fingers found his hole. Oozing ointment, and well-fucked, the pink slot parted easily for three of them as they slowly dug into him.

"You like those big black fingers up your vo-lup-tuous white ass, don't you? Don't you?"

"I like it! I really like it!"

They had nearly another hour to kill, and both cowboys intended on making the best of it. The very best of it.

TWO WORLDS
By Jay Starre

Kennedy's hard-on strained against the fly of his shorts as he chattered on about himself. It throbbed and leaked every time Ricardo's golden eyes met his and that unique ghost of a smile curled his upper lip. His sepia-brown complexion, warm brown arms and smooth dark thighs glowed in the waning desert light washing over him through the big kitchen windows.

"I spoke Korean growing up. My Mom spoke it to me most of the time, and my grandparents almost always used it instead of English. They owned a Korean grocery store in Central L.A. and babysat me nearly every day when both my parents were at work. My father talked to me in English, but he traveled a lot and wasn't around much. Still, by the time I reached school age I had good English. I ended up being an A student, and if you know anything about Koreans, that's very important."

Ricardo was busy preparing them a meal in his small kitchen but managed to turn and nod to Kennedy, letting him know in his quiet way to continue.

As his own dark brown orbs focused on the swell of Ricardo's solid ass, he admitted something about himself he rarely ever told anyone.

"Sometimes I feel like I didn't know what I am. My mother, my grandparents, cousins and all my friends growing up in my neighborhood were other Koreans. My father, a tall and quiet Black dude from L.A. himself, had no relatives, at least that he had anything to do with. I grew up with no sense of myself as Black."

Arriving at that admission in Ricardo's kitchen behind his isolated garage on the Navaho Reservation in northwest Arizona had not been part of the plan he'd launched himself into a few days earlier. His road trip to the southwest during spring break in his junior year at UCLA was supposed to be a journey of discovery. College itself had been a real eye-opener. Virtually everyone he met considered him Black, not Korean. Once he told them he was half-Korean, though, they could easily spot the racial characteristics he'd inherited from that side of his family.

His large and luminous eyes were deep brown and wide-set with just a touch of the slant associated with Asian ethnicity. His nose and mouth were large but had a delicacy to them softened by his Korean heritage. His face was rather broad and flat. His skin was a uniform dark chocolate brown and without blemish. Even his body reflected that mixed heritage. Although he was tall and broad-shouldered like his father, he was lean and almost willowy otherwise.

His first discovery on that journey to Arizona was that the Navaho Nation was big. Almost the same size as the state of West Virginia, it is the largest Indian Reservation in the States. Exploring the desert was his goal that spring. He imagined he would have some time for self-reflection in the barren landscape.

His impressive plans were sabotaged almost as soon as he arrived on the Reservation. His convertible, a gift from his father when he graduated from high school with honors, broke down.

The look of the garage he'd been towed to was not encouraging. At first sight, with shabby wooden walls and peeling paint, the place looked deserted. Then he noticed it was tidy, more than expected of a working garage, and the dude who came out to greet him was quietly self-assured and looked competent.

He couldn't have been much older than Kennedy. He shook his hand and nodded, a hint of a smile showing white teeth in a sepia-brown complexion. It seemed unlikely he wasn't a Navaho, as you had to be a member of the tribe to live on the Reservation. But something about him looked a little different, at least according to Kennedy's expectations.

The look of curiosity on his face must have been evident.

"I'm Ricardo, and I'm half Mexican. My Dad is a big city dude from Nogales. That's what's confusing you. But I am a Navaho. A real live Indian, if you're looking for one."

The ghost of a smile remained in place, along with the firm handshake, which lasted much longer than necessary. Kennedy's cock, always quick to respond, swelled in his shorts. This dude was very interesting, and very sexy. He was a little on the short side, more than half a foot shorter than the six-four Kennedy, and had a stocky, well-built body. The college junior liked that. So did his rising cock. The direct gaze, firm handshake and subdued smile really affected him. The warm brown skin was a turn-on, and the notion they were both half-breeds added to the sense of connection he felt. He rarely felt such an instant link with a total stranger.

"I've got time now. I'll check out your car and see what's up with it. You can watch, or you can sit a spell and take in the scenery."

"I haven't got a clue about mechanical crap. I'll take in the scenery and await your verdict."

He sat just outside the open garage door on a wooden bench in the shade. It was late March and not yet too hot in the northern Arizona hinterland. But the sun was intense that morning and the shade felt good. The view was stunning.

Wild flowers painted the rolling plain with a kaleidoscope of brilliant color. The contrast between the eye-popping brilliance and the reddish sand of the desert floor was breath-taking. The sky was a soft blue with no hint of clouds. The horizon seemed a million miles away.

He'd arrived just in time for that short burst of desert flowering, which apparently lasted only a few weeks after the spring rains. He hadn't planned it, and had to laugh as he contemplated the totally unplanned course of events so far.

He turned to check out the young mechanic and noted he was hard at work with his head buried under the open hood of his car. Frayed cut-off jeans clung to a solid can that jutted out from his waist in a round swell. Sweet!

Again Kennedy had to chuckle. He was about as likely to get a piece of that tail as he was to find out his car could be fixed in ten minutes for ten bucks. The dude did seem interested in him, but he looked straight as hell and a little too macho to offer up his butt for Kennedy's rather massive black cock. It took a real hungry bottom to appreciate its impressive length and the way he loved to pump it balls-deep.

"It's not a big deal. A faulty belt that's gotta be replaced. The only problem is I don't have it in stock and have to order it. Delivery won't be until the morning."

"Yikes. Where can I stay around here for the night?"

He looked around at the lonely road heading back the way he had come and into the empty landscape north in the opposite direction. He'd only seen two cars pass by in the last half hour.

"I've got a place behind the garage. If you're not picky, you can crash on my couch tonight. No charge," he added with a wink and that wisp of a smile.

"Wow. Cool. I'm not in a hurry to get anywhere. I'll just go for a hike around here then while you work. I won't get in your way."

"There's a trail back that way that leads to an interesting arroyo. Just stay on the trail and take some water with you. And your cell phone. Here's my number just in case you get into trouble."

The dude was just too nice. Kennedy was liking him an awful lot and couldn't help fantasizing about what might take place later on that couch of his once they were stripped down for bed.

His mind turned to the world around him as he headed out for his hike. He felt as if he was totally alone in the world. Not another human being was in sight as the lonely garage disappeared behind him.

It wasn't long before he noticed signs of life. Birds flitted among the flowers and landed to rest on the saguaro cactus that reared up here and there. A hawk soared overhead. Bees and other insects swarmed the colorful blooms. A rabbit popped up out of nowhere and hopped out of sight almost as quickly.

The arroyo was worth the walk. Cut from the surrounding plain by years of thunderstorm flooding, it was a red gash in the world and boasted a tiny stream in the bottom. He found his way down and sat by the water for more than an hour, thinking about almost nothing.

Eventually, his thoughts returned to the sexy mechanic. He couldn't help himself and fished out his cock. It reared up instantly in his hand, growing and growing until it was at full mast. It rose up to its full length, dark brown and leaking in the bright light. He pumped it idly as he thought of Ricardo and that round butt of his. How he'd love to slide the throbbing pole between those firm cheeks, seek out the hole, and push it deeper and deeper and deeper.

His cock was a blessing and a curse. It was just too damn long – it actually reached up to his navel! Once he even managed to bend down enough to get the head in his mouth. Problem was, most dudes just couldn't take it all the way, either in their throat or up their ass. And he really, really liked to bury it home.

So much for self-examination, he thought as he pumped it one more time before putting it away. By the time he returned to the garage, it was almost evening. Ricardo was still at work, but when Kennedy came in, he wiped his hands clean on a rag and nodded. "Why don't we eat something? Enchiladas and beans, OK?"

That subdued smile was so engaging, Kennedy had to laugh out loud. "Hell yeah. I can do the dishes if you can cook."

They chatted easily for close to an hour while Ricardo cooked and they ate. Both had lived radically different lives so far, but had one big thing in common.

"We're half-breeds, and don't quite know which world we fit in," Kennedy said.

"You got that right. Come on, let's go outside and sit for a while."

The sun had set while they ate. Just out the back door an old sofa was pushed against the wall and covered with an authentic Navaho blanket. "My aunt made it. She sells them to tourists like you," Ricardo said.

They sat there while Kennedy took in the night sky. It was like nothing he'd ever seen before. The only light came from the front of the garage well behind them. Stretching to infinity was a sparkling universe of stars.

"It's pretty easy to see how the Navaho conjured up all our creation myths out of a sky like that."

Kennedy had no words. He was so far from L.A. it seemed he was on another planet, in another galaxy. That's when a hand settled in his lap. He turned in the darkness to meet a soft mouth pressing lightly against his own.

They kissed. It was gentle at first, as were the tentative hands they explored each other with. That didn't last.

The L.A. college boy was so surprised and happy just to relax there under the stars and make-out, he wasn't as aggressive as usual. Normally, he would have jammed his tongue deep, quickly stripped his playmate, and then gone for his cock and ass. He liked it hot and heavy.

But this dude was different. He had come to really like him in just the short time since they'd met. Liking him didn't make him want to fuck any less, on the contrary he wanted to fuck Ricardo even more than he might otherwise. It was just that he wanted to savor the moment, every moment of whatever transpired.

Marcus Anthony

Ricardo seemed to feel the same. His tongue tickled Kennedy's lips, then slowly explored between them. Kennedy returned the favor, sliding his fat tongue into the Navaho's wet mouth with gentle strokes.

It was Ricardo who first dared to slide a hand into Kennedy's lap and feel the throbbing length of his stiff meat. He gasped around the tongue in his mouth and squeezed that boner before he slowly began to unbutton the fly.

Kennedy's heart pounded as his cock was released and the nimble mechanic's fingers took it in hand. He lurched up off the couch into those slowly stroking fingers and finally found the initiative to return his attentions.

Both his big hands went to work. One hand dove into Ricardo's lap and the other ran down his wide back and down to his ass where he shoved it past the loose waistband and into the warm crack.

Still kissing, Ricardo got up on his knees in the darkness and quickly unbuttoned his own fly. He shoved down on his shorts and underwear then straddled Kennedy. Bent at the waist, he kissed him while pumping his cock. His ass reared out behind him with Kennedy's hand buried in the divide between the firm cheeks.

It was an amazing butt – hairless and solid with a really deep ass valley, and warm and slightly sweaty. Kennedy had to fuck it! But first, he had to eat it.

He broke the kiss and stared up at the dark figure hovering over his lap. There was no way to make out more than a patch of darkness against the stars. He didn't care. "I want to lick your ass. Is that OK?"

"Go for it. And I'll suck your cock," Ricardo answered, following up his soft words with a chuckle.

Kennedy smiled in the darkness as they changed positions on the couch. He was glad to hear the quietly serious mechanic laugh. Hopefully, he'd be making him do more than that soon enough.

163

Ass settled over his face as he lay on his back. They couldn't see the color of each other's skin, dark on dark, and for the first time in both their lives, it didn't seem as if color mattered. Touch and smell and sound were all emphasized by the lack of light.

He felt the warm ass with his hands and smelled the masculine scent of crack as it came down over his nose and lips. He inhaled deeply before he pressed his lips against that smooth valley and began to kiss it.

Ricardo wriggled gently, positioning himself so that his puckered hole found those big wet lips and rubbed against them. Kennedy groaned as the hole blossomed outward against his lips, then kissed back as he began to gently suck on it.

That's when lips settled over the tapered crown of his cock. Lightly sucking, those moist lips encased the head and suckled with little smacks and slurps. After a delicious moment of that, they began so slide downward, a little at a time.

Kennedy was so excited, he could barely contain himself. He wanted to drive his hips upward and ram his cock between the teasing lips – but restrained himself. Instead, he settled down into the couch with his thighs open and relaxed.

He focused on that pouting hole. Sucking harder, he felt the inner flesh surge open and immediately took advantage. His tongue slid into the warm cavern. Ricardo's solid body jerked, and his ass sank down deeper over Kennedy's face. He was definitely enjoying that tongue!

He twisted and stabbed. Ricardo mewled around the cock in his mouth and wriggled over Kennedy's face. His lips settled slowly deeper over the black cock in his mouth. Kennedy immediately understood the connection.

He used his fingers to pull open the young Navaho's hole and dug deeper. His tongue burrowed far up the quivering chute. He got the response he hoped for. Ricardo's mouth slithered farther down his cock, engulfing half of it. Drool oozed from his lips to coat the rest of the lengthy shaft, and he used his fingers to stroke the pulsing black column.

Kennedy could hardly stand it. It was difficult to surrender control, but Ricardo's gentle yet uninhibited manner called for an equal response, out of sheer politeness at least. Besides, his tongue assault obviously was working!

He stretched the lips of Ricardo's pouting hole open wider and stabbed in and out with his tongue. Spit coated it, smearing his big nose, chin and lips. He pulled out his tongue and replaced it with his nose, rubbing it against the wet ass-lips and snorting in ass smell. He replaced his nose with his lips and sucked.

Ricardo squirmed all over, allowing nose, lips and tongue to work over his hole while he paid back the attention by sliding his lips farther and farther down the lengthy pole rearing up from Kennedy's lap. It happened suddenly when it finally did, though. Throat opened up and cock-head slithered into the tight confines. In one smooth glide, Ricardo engulfed the remainder of Kennedy's cock.

It was unbelievable. His balls rubbed up against Ricardo's drooling lips and the entire length of his cock was surrounded by wet warmth. Throat pulsed around his buried cock-head. It was the first time he'd ever been taken so deep.

He groaned and shuddered from head to toe. He sucked voraciously on the young Navaho's tender slot, feeling as if he was melting into the blanket and couch beneath him. It didn't seem as if it could get any better. It did.

With a smack of his lips, Ricardo slowly rose up off the lengthy black cock. When he came to the head, he tickled it with his tongue briefly before reversing direction and sliding back down to eat up all that meat in a single deep gulp.

Kennedy ate ass furiously. He rammed his tongue in and out, twisting and probing. Mouth swallowed him to the root, then slowly reversed and released him. It didn't take long before he felt himself losing control.

He pushed up on Ricardo's ass just enough so he could speak. "If you keep that up much longer, I'm going to shoot, Ricardo," he blurted out.

The young Navaho pulled off with a smack of his lips and chuckled again. "That won't be good. I want this black baseball bat up my ass, especially now that you've turned it inside out with your tongue."

"Hell yeah! You'll have to get some lube, though."

"Coming right up."

Ricardo rose, a dark figure against the starlight. He disappeared briefly, obviously able to navigate his own home in the darkness. Kennedy lay back and caught his breath. He was tempted to stroke his cock, especially now that it was wet and slippery with his new friend's drool, but he was afraid he might shoot if he even touched it.

By the time Ricardo returned, he realized his eyes had grown accustomed to the dim light, and he could actually make out the shadowy form clambering up onto the couch. He reached out for it and found a fat cock thrusting up between smooth thighs. It was much thicker than Kennedy's but certainly couldn't equal his in length.

"Here's the lube."

A bottle was handed to him as he felt Ricardo turn in his hands. There was that firm ass again. He wanted to fuck it so bad! Ricardo got on his hands and knees and wagged that ass against Kennedy's roaming hands.

"It's all yours," he said quietly.

The college student upended the bottle of lube and pressed the end against the top of Ricardo's ass and squirted. The spurt of goo was loud in the silence of the night. He squirted some more, then dropped the bottle onto the couch. Getting up on his knees and leaning forward, he pushed the head of his cock into the deep crack and began to rub it in the slippery mess.

The tip slid down and found the puckered hole. He groaned as he felt the lubed ass-lips gulp at it. Controlling his urge to slam forward, he merely planted it in place and held it there.

But Ricardo was having none of that. With a grunt, he heaved backwards. The tapered crown was swallowed whole by quivering butt-lips. Then almost half the shaft was sucked in.

"Oh my god! Ohhhhhhhhh ... Oh hell yeah! Uhhhhnnnnn ... That feels so fucking great," he muttered between deep sighs.

"You're telling me," Ricardo answered in that subdued voice of his.

Kennedy's cock was slim enough and Ricardo's hole had been teased open by the student's rapacious tongue and lips so that it was no strain for cock to slide into hole. But getting it deep was another matter.

He let Ricardo take charge of that. Kneeling in place, he held firm as the crouching Navaho began to rock back and forth against him. Every push back swallowed up more cock. And more cock.

He reached out and felt that heaving ass with both hands. The skin was smooth and warm. He felt the roundness of the jutting cheeks, then up to the narrow waist. He leaned in and slid his hands around that waist to take hold of cock and balls and massage them. The fat cock throbbed in his hand and the plump nads felt full of spunk as he cupped and fondled them.

His hands moved higher as Ricardo pushed farther back into his lap and swallowed more cock with his greedy asshole. He ran his fingers across the solid abdomen and up to the swell of the firm chest. There too the flesh was warm and smooth. He found the nipples and tweaked them gently.

"Oh yeah. That's so nice. Your cock feels so good deep inside me," Ricardo whispered.

He realized he'd found one of the young Navaho's hot buttons. He continued to tweak and stroke his nipples as Ricardo groaned and heaved with his ass faster and faster. It happened all at once, just like the deep-throating.

His balls slapped up against Ricardo's slippery brown ass-crack. He was buried to the root! He moaned out loud as he felt quivering ass-lips surround the base of his cock and hold tight. This was a first!

"I have to fuck you," he blurted out.

"Go for it," Ricardo answered.

He had held back with commendable restraint. But now he gave in to his urges with a vengeance. He pulled out of that clinging, steamy hole, and then still tweaking those sweet nipples, he rammed home.

"Ohhh! Yeah!"

Ricardo's bleat only encouraged him. Gripping the solid young Navaho by the nipples, he ravaged his oozing hole with that foot-long tool. The hole seemed bottomless and took him in without a hitch. In and out, faster and faster. Lube squished and ass-lips slurped. The slippery friction was merciless. He thought he would blow after only a few minutes of that delicious ride, but strangely, something magical occurred.

He rode that ass like he was riding the stars. In the darkness, it was only the two of them, from totally different worlds yet somehow so much alike. The yielding welcome of that slick hole was like coming home. He buried his cock, yanked it out, and buried it again.

It was Ricardo who was driven to orgasm first. And with good reason. The entire length of that hot rod rammed in and out with rapid-fire intensity. His tender prostate and massaged ass-lips were on fire.

His nipples burned with equal pleasure. The big body embracing him was hot and sweaty and enthralled with him.

"I'm coming. I'm coming with your big black cock up my ass!"

Breathless and grunting, Ricardo shot. Goo splattered Kennedy's fingers where they gripped his nipples. The solid body convulsed in his arms. The hole he fucked went into a series of gripping spasms that rippled all along his thrusting cock.

"Fuck! Me, too!"

He could have gone on much longer, he told himself. But the pleasure of release denied over the past few minutes was too sweet not to surrender to. Cum erupted as he pulled out and sprayed that solid ass with his load.

They rolled over into a face-to-face embrace. Sticky with lube and each other's cum, they pulled the Navaho blanket over them and fell asleep under the stars.

They awoke to the glow of sunrise illuminating their warm brown complexions. Kennedy stared up into the strong features of the half-breed Navaho, reflecting on his own mixed heritage. It really had to be a blessing, if the look Ricardo gave him meant anything. Soft eyes and soft smile and then a gentle kiss told him it was so.

MY OLD KENTUCKY BONE
By Logan Zachary

Logan Zachary (LoganZachary2002@yahoo.com) lives in Minneapolis. His new book Calendar Boys *is out, and his stories can be found in numerous anthologies.*

The crack of the whip hurt my ears as I walked into the barn, but what I saw stopped me in my tracks.

"What the hell are you doing?" I demanded. This was my summer job from college and being a third year social worker, this behavior wasn't tolerated.

Ken loomed over Nick with his whip in hand ready to use it. It looked like a scene from *Gone with the Wind* or *North and South* where the white master is about to whip his slave. This definitely was not to be allowed.

Ken stopped but didn't lower his hand. "Mandingo had it coming."

Nick's wide eyed expression told of another tale.

"Maybe the heat is getting to us, and we're taking on these roles a little too seriously." Psych 101 don't fail me now, I thought. It did look like we had stepped back in time with our costumes for work on.

Nick had on a pair of brown pants held at his waist with a rope and that was all. He was shirtless and bare foot. His ebony skin glistened with sweat as his chiseled body looked as if he had been working in the fields for years. His big hand was still held up in a protected position.

Ken had on suspenders and a button down shirt. His pants were blue and tucked into leather work boots.

I wore a black suit like Rhett Butler wore. Today, I played a gun runner and a bootlegger. I moved over to Nick, and he pushed me behind him. I looked down at his ass, the brown pants hugged his butt like a second skin, and I licked my lips.

"I knew you were on his side, Sam. I just knew it." Ken cracked the whip, and the slender end shot out and slapped Nick's arm. A line of blood rose across his black skin.

Nick's hand shot out like a snake and caught the whip. He wrapped the leather around his wrist and pulled.

Ken was caught off guard and stumbled forward into Nick's arms. "Don't you fucking touch me!"

I stepped behind him. "Ken, you need to calm down."

Sweat beaded on his forehead and trickled down his face. Was he sick? Dehydrated? Crazy from the heat? Wasn't there a study of students who played guards and prisoners and the position of power went to their heads?

The park had shut down, and the Southern Plantation Festival was over for the day. I had needed my back pack from the barn, otherwise I would have been off to supper and wouldn't have walked into this scene.

"Sam, step back, so you don't get hurt," Nick warned. Blood ran down his forearm and soaked into the leather whip as we held Ken in his arms.

"Get away from me, you queer," Ken spat.

How did he know I was gay, flashed through my mind, but then I realized he had been talking about Nick. This muscle bound black god of perfection, gay?

Ken let go of the whip and pushed against Nick with all of his might. He looked around the barn frantically and spotted the pitchfork. His eyes were wild and crazy, and I knew what he was thinking.

I dove for him as he rushed toward the weapon. A wooden harness hung from the rafters and swung in front of me.

Ken's hands hit the wood as he rushed me and slipped through the yoke's loops.

I pulled on the leather straps and trapped his arms. I wrapped the long end around one wrist and then the other, securing him to the yoke. The end had a knot in it, and I pulled it into the notch on the end and locked him into place.

Nick slowly rose to his feet and stood next to me.

"Faggot. Cocksucker," Ken spat at us.

Nick turned to face me and took my head into his large hands. He held them there for a few seconds as his brown eyes stared into my hazel ones. And then he kissed me, long and hard and deep. His tongue entered my mouth and tasted mine.

"See, I knew it," Ken said, pulling on his restraints.

My hands held onto Nick and caressed his strong arms. My hands ran along his muscles and felt the power underneath. None of my psych classes prepared me for this.

Ken kicked at us, and almost made contact with my ass.

Nick looked up into the rafters and followed the rope up to a wooden pulley on the center beam that held the roof up. He loosened the rope and pulled hard on the pulley above us.

Ken rose a foot off the barn floor. His booted feet kicked at the air, instead of the straw.

Nick pulled me over to a pile of straw and motioned for me to lie down. He unbuttoned my black shirt and exposed my sweaty, hairy chest to him. He worked down to my waistband and saw the hair grew thicker as he went lower.

My cock swelled and grew, straining against the tight fabric of my britches. His hand brushed my erection through the pants and send waves of pleasure over me.

Ken spun above us like a manic mobile. "Let me down. Let me down or I'll … I'll …"

Nick's mouth came down on my nipple and sucked it into his mouth. It rose as soon as he touched it, and then he rolled the tender nub between his teeth. His hand slid down my torso and teased about going into my pants.

His other hand untied his rope belt. There was a huge bulge in the front of his brown pants that hadn't been there a moment ago.

I looked over his wedge shaped back and saw his pants slip down off his ass. The most beautiful fleshy orbs of man flesh rose into a crescent moon. A manly, musk rose from him as his tongue trailed down my belly.

Ken stopped yelling as soon as Nick's ass came into his bird's eye view. His pants tented in front as his arousal grew.

My hand slid over Nick's sweaty body and cupped his ass. I could feel the muscles ripple under his skin, so solid, so powerful.

He opened my pants and pulled them down to my knees.

My cock sprang up as the pressure released, and it grew another few inches. A wetness pooled at the tip.

Nick licked my cock through my briefs. His hot breath penetrated to my skin adding to the sweat and heat. He reached back and removed his pants. He tossed them aside and returned to my groin.

I felt a heavy object dangle above one leg as he mouthed my cock.

His fingers massaged my balls and rolled them back and forth.

My hands ran over his bald head and felt the stumble tickle my nerve endings. I guided his head to my dick and gently pushed his head down to give me more pressure, more stimulation.

He reached up and pulled down the elastic on my underwear.

The tip of my cock emerged, and he licked it, tasting the pre-cum that oozed out. He licked down my shaft as he pulled the briefs lower. His tongue trailed to my balls.

I rose up on my hands, so he could pull the underwear off my ass. The straw crunched underneath me and scratched me.

Nick sucked a low hanging ball into his mouth and tried to swallow it. His tongue lapped at it and sent shivers over my body. He picked up my other ball and slipped it into his mouth. He drew down on them as he jacked my cock with his hand.

I felt his other hand explore my ass, his thick, calloused finger touched my tender hole and explored, seeking entrance. I bucked my hips into his face, and he released my balls from his warm mouth.

Nick licked my dick and kissed the mushroom head before he swallowed all eight inches of me. His nose sniffed my pubic bush, ripe from the sweat of the day. "You taste and smell delicious." His finger entered me, slowly, filling me. The rough skin of his hands tingling my hole.

I pushed down on his finger, forcing him to dive deeper into me.

His mouth pulled hard on my cock.

"Oh yes," I moaned, rocking my hips, faster and faster.

"Fuck him good and hard," Ken called from above.

Nick stopped and withdrew his finger from my ass. He sucked hard on my cock, draining any fluid that escaped. He rose and stood over me. His huge cock waved over my head, and I gasped. He looked down at me and smiled. He stroked his uncut twelve inches a few times, milking the sweat and pre-cum off and onto my face.

A drop landed on my lips, and I licked it away immediately, savoring his manly seed and sweat.

Nick turned to face Ken, his amazing black ass flexing as he turned. His powerful, black, and beautiful body sculpted to perfection out of flesh.

Ken gasped as he saw Nick's cock.

Nick walked over to him. "Looks like you're enjoying the show more than you should." He ran his hand up Ken's pant leg and stopped at his fly. He unbuttoned and unzipped, opening the blue pants.

Ken's basket burst out of the V.

Nick pulled his pants down and off. His shoes followed and dropped to the ground.

Ken's underwear tented and bulged.

"Master may I?" Nick asked as he pulled down his briefs.

Ken's seven cock dangled as did the rest of his body.

"Mandingo likes the master's white cock." Nick licked it. "Sweet, but not as nice as fine as his." He pointed to me.

I flushed at his compliment.

Nick walked over to the pitchfork and ran his hand up and down the shaft. "Maybe I should use this on him as he was going to use it on me?"

Ken stopped struggling and watched as Nick approached him.

Nick ran his hand up and between his legs and up to his ass. He looked up into his eyes and slowly pressed the handle between his cheeks.

Ken opened his mouth to say something and stopped as an expression of pleasure came over his face.

Instead of inserting the wooden handle, he slipped a finger into him. Nick's other hand grabbed his dick and started to stroke it. He moved his other hand in and out of his ass. He spun Ken around so I could see his ass.

Nick's hairy ass was tight and firm, a perfect bubble but with Speedo tan lines.

My cock jumped at the sight of his milky, white bottom.

"Do you want to tap this?" He pumped into his butt. "Or do you want this?" He released Ken's cock and grabbed his own massive meat and shook it at me.

A smile came across my face as I considered my options.

"You want both of us, don't you?" Nick asked. He looked up at the harness and the rafters as he considered what he could do. He walked over to the wooden peg and slowly lowered Ken. As his feet touched the ground, Nick warned him, "Don't try anything."

Ken waited as Nick released the rope.

I watched as Nick guided Ken to the half wall and secured the harness to it.

He lifted Ken's shirt and motioned for me to join him.

I admired his two orbs of thick fur.

Nick dropped down to his knees and spread Ken's cheeks wide open. "Let me loosen him up for you." He wiggled his tongue at me and dove for the hairy hole.

Ken arched his back and moaned as Nick's tongue entered him.

I enjoyed the sight of Nick's ass and stepped behind him and rubbed the smooth ebony bootie.

He pushed back at me, encouraging me to enjoy whatever I wanted. He spread his legs wider.

I spooned his ass, as my cock slipped along his crack, and I reached around his torso and found that amazing dick. My fingers weren't able to touch going around his shaft. Running down the length of him, my balls threatened to empty their load across his back.

He pushed back on me, and I felt a thick creamy ooze flow out of his cock into my hand.

"Are you ready?" he asked as he pulled his tongue out of Ken's ass. "I know he is." He stepped to the side and showed me the hairy heaven in front of me. He handed me a condom and ripped open one for himself.

I swallowed hard, as I knew where he planned to insert his massive uncut cock.

He squeezed his dick into the rubber and motioned for me to hurry up.

I followed suit and moved to stand in front of the heavenly, hairy hole. "I need …"

Nick handed me a bottle of lube and showed me his greased pole.

I poured a handful of lubed over my cock and spread it over Ken's crack. I explored his hole; my finger tickled by the hair and guided my lubed cock to the sweet spot.

I slipped the fat head into his pucker and pushed forward.

Ken's ass swallowed my cock as I drove into him all the way. No sooner did my balls slap Ken's butt, did I feel Nick's dick press into me. I felt my opening stretch as my cock slid out. I pushed back on the Mandingo, inch by inch he filled me.

I surged forward into Ken, and Nick followed deeper into me. I thought I'd split in two, but the hot hairy hole my cock entered pulled me deeper. I thrust in and my ass relaxed, pain became pleasure, and it took over. I increased my rate and reached around Ken to his dick. My hands anchored me there, as I pulled on him. His hairy balls spilled over my hands as I stroked down his shaft.

Pre-cum flowed out of Ken and made my hand slip faster and easier on him, our rhythm increased as I bounced between the two men.

Nick licked up my neck and nibbled on my ear lobe.

I turned my head, giving him better access.

His tongue's tip entered my ear, and I felt my balls rise. I thrust forward and the pendulum swing of my testicles bounced off Ken's ass.

Nick doubled his speed, and I matched his rate.

Ken moaned in pleasure. His balls pulled up, and his cock shot out its load. His thick cream shot between my fingers and hit the half wall.

As I felt his load flow, my balls released and filled my condom. My whole body tensed, and my ass puckered and sucked down hard on Nick. I felt his cock swell as the wave of his cum ran down his shaft and exploded out of the end. Heat filled my ass, as my balls sent another wave out into Ken.

I slammed harder into him and felt another orgasm shoot out of him. He pushed back against me, his ass milking more and more out of me.

Nick's cock pulsated inside of me and sent the sensory overload into my cock, making it too tender to touch.

I pulled out of Ken and knocked Nick onto his ass. His cock slammed deeper into me, and my prostate shot out another load.

Nick held me on his dick as my body vibrated.

I rolled off of him and covered my ass with both hands. I lay in a heap as my body returned to normal.

Nick crawled over to me and touched my leg. "Are you okay?"

"That was amazing," I said.

Nick cradled me in his arms, and we lay there for a few minutes.

"Hey guys. Can you untie me?" Ken asked. He snapped his fingers.

His hairy ass smiled at us as we sat up.

"Why is he so calm?" I asked.

Nick laughed.

"Why are you laughing?"

"Do you want to tell him or should I?" Ken asked.

"What?"

"We kind of set you up." Nick said.

"What? I don't understand."

"We planned to set you up and see what happened." Ken laughed.

"You didn't attack Nick?"

Ken shook his head. "No, I figured you are studying to be a social worker, fighting for truth and justice and the American way, so I knew you'd rescue him and maybe we'd get to see you naked. Never in my wildest dreams did I think this would happen."

I stood up and slapped his ass.

"Hey," he yelled.

"And I thought you were my friend." I turned to Nick.

"You are, I just wanted to be friendlier, and I didn't know how to break you out of your shell. I guess we found out." Nick stood and held out my underwear. "You were amazing."

I stepped into my briefs as I searched for my pants.

Nick jumped up and caught me. "I'm sorry. I didn't mean to hurt you. I just wanted to … get naked with you and have some fun."

"Whatever," I pulled on my shirt.

"Ken, help me," Nick said.

"I'm a little tied up here," he said.

I turned to look at his perfect, hairy ass.

"How can you say no to that?" Nick asked. He framed Ken's ass with his hands, and then he held his penis out to me. "Or this?"

"Damn, you're right." I bent over and kissed the wet tip of his dick. "So my question to you guys is …"

"Yes?" Nick asked.

"When can we do this again?"

Nick slipped into his pants and said, "When we get to your place."

"Okay." And we headed out of the barn.

"Hey guys, are you going to untie me? Guys?" Ken yelled to us. "It was my idea."

COCKY
By Landon Dixon

Landon Dixon's writing credits include the magazines Men, Freshmen, *and* Mandate; *numerous anthologies; and the short story collection,* Hot Tales of Gay Lust.

I stared at his cock laid out on my desk. It was enormous, long and thick and ... unerect!

I blew out my cheeks like Dizzy Gillespie hitting the high notes on the world's largest trumpet, breathed, "I see why you'd like to keep it."

He was standing in front of my desk, cock lying out in front of him, in front of me. I couldn't take my bugged-out eyes off the coal-black, vein-ribboned, awesome appendage. A client had never dropped a cocky calling card like that on me before, and I'd been in the dick (detective) racket for years.

"Two men have already threatened to cut it off," he blubbered. "Feed it to me."

It was the kind of chow I'd spend a fortune to feast on any day of the week and twice on Sunday. But I tried to slap a professional demeanor on my mug, blinking and gulping away the look of utter astonishment, and unabashed lust. "I-I charge five hundred dollars a day for a ... guard job like this. Including nights."

I glanced up momentarily, at his boyish, black-as-night features. He'd said his name was Lawrence Denkins, twenty years old, that he was new in the big northern city, originally hailing from the deep south sticks. He had a slight Dixie accent, all right, a true southern gentleman's gamecock. He said he was being threatened by some unscrupulous types, men trying to take advantage of his native innocence and nurtured endowment. He needed his shadowed dick shadowed, protected from foul play, and I was just the dick-lover for the job.

"That's satisfactory," he said with a smile.

He was wearing a white T-shirt and pair of blue jeans, white runners. His dark hair was cut short, his face kind of chubby and round, body long and lean. His big, wide eyes were as black as his skin, gleamed the same. My shining eyes dropped back down, along his cock that was the stuff of porn legends and squirt dreams.

I just had to get closer, more hands-on with the subject of my investigation. "I, uh, should take a closer look," I babbled, gesturing with my eyes, "to better know what I'm protecting."

"Sure, help yourself," Lawrence obliged.

I swallowed dry as a gulch, staggered around my desk, up to the young man with the over-mature organ. He pivoted, sliding his sledge off the creaking desk and flopping it around to meet me like the trunk of an African elephant. I went down on my knees, which wouldn't support me anymore anyway.

His cock draped out of his open fly like a tube of molassified dough; to be pulled and kneaded and needed and stroked into a shape even firmer and longer and stronger. And I was just the doughboy to do it. I laced my shaking fingers around the middle of the bulging shaft and lifted the flexible pipe up to my beaming brown face.

"Oh!" Lawrence gasped softly, encouragingly.

I'm medium-height, medium-build, battle-tested and almost shockproof after ten long years in the PI racket. I've seen a lot of things, handled a lot of different cases, but I'd never seen nor handled anything like this before. Lawrence's weighty dong throbbed in my medium-sized hand, testing every sinew of my gripping mitt, straining every fiber in my groping mind. As I held the hose up to the blazing light of my glaring green eyes, thinking, *he's not heavy, he's my brother.*

And then my pounding heart skipped ten or twelve beats, as I felt the black mamba thicken, lengthen, engorge, and rise, hot blood rushing between my fingers and filling the veins, hot blood rushing to my dizzy head. Lawrence's mammoth man-meat was pulsating out pole-like in my clasping, widening hand.

"That feels good, Mr. Page," he murmured, reminding me there was a personality attached to that mighty impressive penis.

"Thomas. Call me Thomas," I rasped, breathing humid awed reverence onto that seizing-up snake.

My inspection got more physical. I dragged my hand up, along, the bloating hot shaft, taking a stroke; then another, and another, and another. By the twenty-seventh such warm, worshipping, full-palm and stretched-finger caress, Lawrence's cock had fully returned my affection, jutting out a mind-boggling, mouth-watering length right in front of me. I was stunned like a tailgater at a sausage factory, staring at, feeling the tremendous size and coursing power of that foot-long mahogany log.

"You can use two hands, if you like."

I liked. I had two hands.

I clenched over-inflated shaft with both sweaty, trembling paws, pumped with the pair. Lawrence was jerked back and forth with the force of my tug, his clean-cut, boiled-up shaft pulsing in my hands. I gazed into the gaping slit adorning his deep-purple, mushroomed hood, and I knew to fully wrap my mind around his case I just had to wrap my lips around his cock. "I-I need to get a taste, the true flavor ..."

"Be my guest."

I almost leapt up and clicked my knees together. Accommodating clients were the best. I double-pumped some more, then double-clutched. Then I spread my plush, mocha mouth flaps as wide apart as they would go, and then some, fed my cavernous, red, cauldron-like craw super-swelled beefy cockhead. I took Lawrence's thunder cap into my mouth and sealed my lips, barely, around it.

"Oooh, Mr. Thomas!" he cooed.

I reveled in the meaty texture and massive size of all that cushiony hood cramming my mouth, staring cross-eyed along the vast length of asphalt-shaded shaft that stretched onto infinity out of my mouth, that was left to be consumed. Only a professional sword-swallower with a taste for the gay things in life could've done that dong full justice, I knew. My tongue explored the twin split glans of the perfectly-formed, bodaciously-apportioned cockhead, my lips tugging like a babe's on its mother's over-swollen nipple.

Lawrence's cock vibrated in my hands and mouth, in tune to his body.

I pushed my head forward, slid my hands downward, swallowing more colossal cock. Dong filled my manhole of a mouth, gliding in between my raw lips, an endless supply of succulent meat. I gulped shaft until cap hit the back of my throat all too quickly, and I gagged slightly, with delight, and defeat. Two-thirds of that nightstick still stretched out before my mouth.

I billowed my bloated cheeks, sucking on Lawrence's cock, pumping it with my hands, pulling on the young man's amazing appendage. The taste was throbbing hard rubber, with a salty drip at the tip. My mouth muscles threatened to rupture, lips to tear, hands to carpal, mind to break, as I sucked and pumped harder and faster, bobbing my gourd in a frenzy, pistoning my paws.

Lawrence groaned, thrust. His huge, hairless black balls burst out of the zipper of his jeans, at the base of his boner, and their overlarge size told me I was going to get a double-normal serving of joy jizz. *Bring on the flood!* I mentally bellowed, sucking ferociously, pumping furiously.

"I'm-I'm …!"

He didn't have to finish the thought, just the action. I rolled my glassy eyes up at the guy and piped sheer ecstasy on his beautiful boy-face. His eyes were squeezed shut and his teeth gritted together, fists clenched and body rigid. Then he jerked, jolted, and I tasted his full rapture, spouting down my throat.

His monster cock surged and spasmed in the cramped, heated, drooling wet confines of my mouth, in my death-gripping hands. A blast of spicy sperm coated the back of my throat, another, another, another, another, another, and another.

My gag-reflex was drowned in a steamy sea of semen, swamping me. My mouth and hands wrestled to keep the jerking, jacking python spewing inside me, keep sucking and gulping and pumping.

But while Lawrence's propensity for prick and jism was immense, my appetite for cock and ball-batter was even vaster. I took every hosing dose of sperm he gave me from his giant cock – gratefully, to the last sucked and squeezed drop.

# # # # #

We were going out to lunch (he wanted to eat; I wasn't hungry), when the first assailant appeared. We'd just stepped out of the building and onto the sidewalk, when a tall, sharply-dressed man suddenly flung himself at Lawrence's crotch, yelling, "When are you going to pay me for all the clothes I got you!?"

I chopped him on the back of the neck before his long fingers and elegant hands could land on the valuable and voluble package in Lawrence's jeans. The guy folded up like a cheap suit, planting his aquiline nose into the concrete.

There he lay, beating the sidewalk with his slender fists and whining more plaintively than his demand for cash, "Why wouldn't you fuck me!? Why wouldn't you fuck me!?"

I hustled Lawrence away.

The second attempt on the young man's crotch occurred the next morning. Lawrence stayed at my apartment overnight, for his safety and my satisfaction. I'd wanted to get the lad lubed and lunging into my ass with his man-skewer – to gain a real appreciation for the depths of his issues – but he'd put me off, stuffed my mouth and throat again instead. And we were walking down the street to a diner for a late breakfast (my treat, though I still wasn't hungry), when a huge man in a checked suit loud enough to wake the neighborhood suddenly charged at the nether regions I'd been sworn to protect and uphold.

He bellowed, "Where's that car I lent you!?" Right before my bladed hand bounced off his bull neck with no effect.

Fortunately, I'd pulled Lawrence aside at the same time, and his attacker ran face-first into the side of the building. As the guy slumped to the sidewalk in a crumpled heap of color, he moaned, "I just wanted you to fuck me! I just wanted you to fuck me!"

Continuing the common theme of the last two days.

I rushed Lawrence away from the scene of the collision.

I sucked him off after breakfast in a back alley, then blew him like Lena's horn in the shower back at my apartment after dinner (the food and fellatio again both my treats). The all-protein diet was doing wonders for my figure and skin, but not my disposition; I yearned, pined, lusted for Lawrence to lard his tool into my ass, blast me to kingdom come. But he wouldn't oblige.

So, while he lay sleeping the satiated sleep of the ball-drained, well-fed, and rent-free in my bed for a second night, I slipped out and did what I was trained, and normally paid, to do: dig up some answers to some questions.

# # # # #

Lawrence stumbled out of my bedroom around noon, rubbing the deep sleep and self-satisfaction out of his eyes. And then those innocent-looking peepers widened, and he stopped in his tracks, his tropical vine dangling between the slim stalks of his legs.

"Good morning," I said. "Recognize any of these gentlemen?"

There were five of us standing in the middle of my living room, naked: Allan Kalule, the tall tailor; Donovan Grimshaw, the hulking car dealer; Titus Montgomery, the short-order restaurateur; Briscoe Kane, the blinged-up jeweler; and yours truly, the tricky dick. It hadn't taken me long to track down the trail of unhinged jaws, unplugged assholes, and mountainous debts that Lawrence had left behind him during his short time in the city. For a supposedly wide-eyed, fresh-cocked kid from the country, he'd used the oldest trick in the dirty business book: shaking his third leg for big payouts, orally teasing material goods out of good gay men with the promise of ultimate anal.

"Time to pay the pipers, Lawrence," I said. "We want our pound of flesh."

He took a step back, gulping, cock twitching.

"Up the ass," I added unnecessarily.

He claimed he hadn't wanted to hurt any of us, anally, was going to pay us all back, eventually. But it was put out and shut up time. We five grinned like a pack of wolves about to get it doggy-style from Black Fang, while Lawrence grinned back, sheepishly.

I spun the couch around with the force of four eager helpers, and we all lined up against it, gripping the back, bending our backs and thrusting out our backsides. We watched Lawrence heft his slab of blood sausage, get it all hard and jutting with some sensual hand strokes, then grease it all gleaming with enough lube to equip an orgy porn set. Five sets of eyes and five individual brown eyes watched and waited, anxious to feel, to experience all that man-meat stuffing our anuses, churning our chutes.

Lawrence knew who he owed the most, and at five hundred dollars a day for only two days I wasn't the lucky stiff to get lustily stiffed first. That honor went to Donovan, the burly automobiler. Lawrence gripped one of the man's huge, chocolate buttocks with one hand, his huge, ebony cock with the other, then thrust forward, piling shining fat cap up against pucker, pushing and pushing and pushing, punching through.

Donovan's roar of delight made the walls wobble, Lawrence shoving his entire club up the man's ass, lunging bone home. Then the young man gripped both of Donovan's wide hips and pumped his, finally delivering on the teasing, tantalizing, terrible-terrific promise of penis-extreme penetration he'd made, and reneged on, to all of us. Donovan hollered ecstasy after only a few heated thunder-strokes, his own spearing erection spewing all on its own.

The country boy with the city smarts and horse-like tool went down the line, hitting and humping Briscoe's black ass, Allan's tan butt, Titus' dusky derriere. He filled and fucked them all, fucked them hard. The hot smack of clenched thighs against rippling buttocks filled the air. Along with the sharp scent of flung sweat, the musky aroma of flapping sacks, the cloying smell of spurting cum; the awesome squelching and sucking sounds of enormous, steel-hard cock stoking burning holes.

I trembled in anticipation, dick vibrating, taking it all in. And then taking it all-in.

"Stick your big, hard, gorgeous, black cock up my ass, Lawrence!" I growled, thrusting out my butt.

He grinned, his ass-ram glistening. Since I was the one who'd cracked the case of the petulant penis, he'd saved his semen for me.

I felt his hand on my cheek, pulling me open. Then his knob on my pucker, pressing to pop in. I bit my lip and strangled the sofa; and then swelled twice my size with pleasure, as Lawrence busted his cap into my ass and bloated my chute.

I pushed back, he pushed forward. What seemed like cord after cord of hardwood filled my anus and soul, pumping me up to the heavens.

"Fuck!" I hissed, stuffed to the gills. I gulped, expecting to taste cock in my throat.

Lawrence gripped me, ripped me, pounding his pole back and forth in my chute. My ass and body and brain blazed with the utter, absolute anal fulfillment. I tore a hand off the couch and grabbed onto my own frozen cock, fisted.

"I'm sorry!" Lawrence bleated. "I shouldn't have strung you guys along! I should've ..."

He couldn't go on with his dickfelt apology. Because just then he bucked, blasted my ravaged ass with blistering hot semen. Showing, not telling, his true sexual contrition in steaming loads.

I arched up onto my toes, quivering out of control. My cock exploded in my shunting hand, sending semen spraying against the sofa (I really should've put down a plastic drop-cloth). As Lawrence rammed full-bore into my reamed rectum, dousing my bowels with superheated spurt after spurt; my own brutal orgasm shaking the foundations of my consciousness, and the building.

Lawrence still gets his food, clothing, cars, jewelry, and protection services on the house – honestly, on the end of his tremendous organ slamming our asses. A fair exchange between cocky and cocked.

MEAT LOVERS
By Landon Dixon

I can't pass a pizza joint, smell the pies baking, without thinking of the wild times I had with DeShawn at Doughboys.

I was just coming off a bitter divorce (that's the thing about legalized marriage for same-sex couples in Canada; there's also legalized divorce). Ryan had taken the house, the money, and my dignity, and I was left looking for any kind of job I could scrounge up to pay the rent on the crummy apartment-motel room I was rotting away in. So when I saw a sign up in the window of Doughboys, I applied.

It was just a small, independent, neighborhood pizza place, with a mediocre product and a menace of a boss. The guy who owned the business, Lugo Brasso, worked full-time as an asshole, never fell below expectations of meeting it.

He interviewed me, asked me how low I'd go to get the job. He was talking wages, not sucking his dick. I'd rather have sucked his dick, if it'd meant at least minimum wage. But he provided the beater for me to drive, and I accepted the job as pizza delivery boy. Even though I was thirty, still had some twinkle in my brown eyes, some spring left in my long-legged step.

Everybody else (the cooks, the other drivers, the rats that hung around the dumpster out back) hated Lugo, too. And they were always inventing ways to get back at the guy. We'd steal meat and vegetables, crust and cardboard and vice versa. The cooks would bake extra pies into an order for themselves, with a slice-off to the drivers. Everyone would goof off as much as possible, piss in Lugo's coffee pot until he started bringing it from home.

The customers weren't much better than the boss. It was a working poor neighborhood, and tips were as scarce as teeth, fights over orders as common as empties in the alleys. Some drivers bragged about banging the occasional customer, but from what I saw, both men and women, you'd have to be pretty damn hungry to stick your salami in any hole except for the one in the fence around the local construction site.

DeShawn was working the ovens one night when he called me over. "Just got an order from the two old ladies on Roseberry. The ones who always want the special items and then still bitch when they get them."

I nodded, wearily. "They've given me more abuse and less money than Lugo most of the time."

DeShawn grinned, evilly. "Well, tonight I'm going to put a little extra seasoning in their mozzarella."

I stared at the short, Afro'ed guy, as he slid an unbaked sixteen-inch closer on the back counter. Then I gaped, when he unzipped his jeans, pulled out his dick, started stroking.

"Hey, DeShawn, come on!"

"That's exactly what I'm trying to do, buddy," he grunted, pulling pud harder.

I glanced through the opening in the wall between the kitchen and storefront. Nobody there. It was late, the streets dark and deserted. I looked back down at DeShawn's cock, and was startled to see how much it'd grown in just those few seconds.

The thing was poling out hard and long, long, long in his tugging hand. DeShawn's a good-looking guy, with bright brown eyes and full black lips and a tight, toned body. And now I was seeing the real attraction of the man – his eight-inch cock. He had it stoked full-length, shaft vein-ribboned and swollen thick, hood bloated purple, slit pointing ominously at the pizza pie.

I swallowed hard. I'd always thought the guy was straight, but now I wasn't so sure. Was this really a gruesome prank on the gruesome twosome, or was this some sort of seductive snake dance he was performing for my benefit?

I didn't know what to do. So I just watched. And that was plenty pleasurable in itself.

He grinned at me, shifting his hand up and down his enormous slab of meat. His balls hung out of his zipper in the shadow of his dong, big and hairy and dangling. His small hand was sure and strong, stroking tight and quick, wrist flicking as he reached cap, pulling in sensual rhythm. And when he pulled up his white T-shirt, slid his other hand up his ridged, dusky stomach, his fingers onto a pointing, licorice nipple, I almost lost my self-control.

DeShawn groaned, rolling a stiffened bud, wanking his stiffened cock. He looked at me with hooded eyes, erotically jerking himself off right in front of me. I licked my lips and glared, the pull of meat strong in myself, as well.

A car slowed on the street out front. I shot a glance that way. The car drove on. DeShawn pumped his cock even faster, harder, fisting now, from balls to cap, stretching his noir pipe, biting his lip and grunting. The phone rang, and rang, and rang.

"Fuck!" he cried, bucking.

I just about brushed the pizza aside and took its place on my knees, to take DeShawn's hot cock-spurts in the face, and mouth. But somehow I controlled myself, as DeShawn lost control.

He was jolted by orgasm, his dick spearing up in his pumping hand. Semen burst out of his slit, a heated white rope of it, splashed down on the pie. Followed by another jet, and another. I wanted to wrap my arms around the shaking guy and take hold of his hose. But I still wasn't sure of his bent, and I didn't want a bloody nose to go with my bloody job.

So I watched in awe, as he sprayed out a heaping topping of sperm onto the pizza, jerking with joy. Until he finally hit empty, and then wiped and tucked his massive, spent organ back into his jeans, paddled the pie into the oven.

I didn't get one complaint from the two old ladies on Roseberry. In fact, they gave me a four-bit tip, just based on the fresh-baked, fresh-caked smell of their pizza. I took the long way back to the store, relieving myself of the pressure DeShawn had built up in my balls along the way.

# # # # #

Nothing seemed to come of DeShawn letting me watch him come until two weeks later, when a family of ten kids and two sets of parents sent back the eight pies I'd tried to deliver to them, the order righteously screwed up.

"Hey, DeShawn!" I yelled, storming into the joint through the back door. "You gave me four extra-large vegetarians and four extra-large meat lovers, when the order was six extra-large pepperoni and mushrooms and two large shrimp and anchovies! What the hell's going on!? What the hell am I supposed to do with these pizzas!?"

"Shove 'em up your ass and have a party, for all I care!" he shot back, working the paddles and ovens like a madman, sweat filming his face in the blast-furnace heat.

It was Friday night, payday for the neighborhood, and the orders were flooding in like cheap booze. "You took this order, didn't you!?"

He loaded an oven with a couple of large meat lovers, then grabbed the slip of paper out of my hand. "No fuckin' way! It was Lugo, that fuckin' moron! He's working the phone and driving himself tonight, since Glen phoned in sick."

I dropped the stack of tepid pies down on the counter. "Well, that's just cheesy! He's probably got the pizzas I need."

DeShawn smirked, wiping his dark forehead with a floury hand. "Why don't you go chasing after his hairy ass? Maybe grab yourself a slice."

I was hot, too, and that 'crack' set me right off. I ripped the lid off a meat lover and dug my hand inside, scooped up a mittful of toppings and sauce and flung them at DeShawn.

I don't know what I was thinking. I guess I wasn't. But sometimes acting impulsively has the most unintendedly sexy consequences.

The fistful of pizza hit DeShawn square in the mush, splashed all over his handsome mug. He yelped, parted the slop with his hands so he could see. Then he whipped a box off the stack and opened it up and loaded up and let fly.

Pizza hit me in the face, warm and gooey. I heaved another handful at him. And the food fight was on.

Boxes were torn open and toppings tossed with a vengeance. Followed by dough, in hurtled hunks and slices. The air was filled with edible missiles. We were splattered with tomato sauce and meat toppings and flour, both of us yelling and laughing wildly.

I grabbed up a couple of fully-load slices and charged DeShawn, smacking him in the face with the pair and rubbing them in. He smeared my pan with a triangular piece of pie, grabbing onto me and squishing the goo into my features. I grasped him with my greasy hands, and we started wrestling, our faces dripping tangy pizza fixings.

I succeeded in pinning his arms behind his back and laughing in his face. And he succeeded in shocking me, by sticking out his tongue and licking sauce right off my cheek.

I stopped struggling then, and stared at the guy, feeling his hot body against mine. He licked me again. And I licked back.

That's when pure sweet Hell really broke loose. We flung our arms around one another and frantically kissed, Frenched, tonguing

197

tongues and lips and cheeks, the frenzy flaming blisteringly erotic. There was no doubt now about DeShawn's orientation. The way he sucked on my tongue almost made me come in my pants.

We peeled off each other's T-shirts, getting bare-chested, wiping our hands all over one another's torsos. DeShawn really knew his way around a man's pecs and nipples, clutching, squeezing, pinching, pulling. I groaned, and he slammed his mouth into mine again, swallowing up my delight, famished as I was.

Our hot cocks pressed together through our jeans, rubbing, squeezing, pulsating. DeShawn dipped his head down and tongued tomato sauce off my right nipple, my left, teasing the buds so stiff they vibrated, his wet, bright-pink sticker making me dance in his arms. Then howl, when he sucked on my nipples, bit into them, chewing on the buzzing bits of meat.

Our jeans got lost in the mayhem. I gripped DeShawn's cock with a slippery hand, and pumped. He groaned, thrusting out his prick, the thing throbbing alive and huge in my stroking hand. I reveled in the feel, the heated beat, the sheer size, as I glided my paw up and down. As DeShawn grabbed up some more spilled pizza and recoated my pecs, ate off of my heaving chest.

We were face to face, glaring at one another, breathing hard. DeShawn got a hot greasy grip on my cock, pumped to my tugging rhythm on his dong. We kissed, tongued, dripping sweat and toppings, pulling hard on each other's meat.

I groaned when DeShawn suddenly let go of my boiling cock. Yelped, when he rolled up a slice of dough into dildo shape and reached around and stuffed it up my ass.

"Yes!" I cried, shooting onto my tip-toes, DeShawn shooting the soft-baked dowel into my anus.

He went deep as he could, then pumped, breathing hot humid air in my face. I tilted my head back and let my mouth hang open, surging

Marcus Anthony

with shimmering heat thanks to that churning crust in my chute, DeShawn fucking my manhole.

I had to reciprocate. The guy was cooking up a storm in my ass and balls, my cock twitching to his secret, sexy ingredient. But I knew I could deliver just as good. So I seized hold of a slice and rolled, squeezing dough and toppings and sauce all together, shoving the pizza dong up DeShawn's butt. My fist pressed into his trembling butt cheeks, the order pushed home in his ass.

We fucked each other with our hand-molded dildos, our cocks kissing hard together, like our lips, bare, overheated bodies banging against one another. We went faster and faster, messy as any ten-topping pie.

"I want to suck you, eat your meat!" I blurted, desperate for a true taste of the man before it was too late.

DeShawn spat in my mouth, thrust his tongue inside and swirled it around. Then pulled the pizza out of my ass. I followed suit.

He cleared a space up on the counter and we climbed aboard. I stretched out flat on my back, DeShawn over top of me, straddling my head with his knees. This was exactly the meaty topping I'd been craving all along, the stud's dong dropping down from his loins into my face, bulbous cap brushing my lips.

I was about to open my big, hungry mouth up wide and consume his beefy cap, when he beat me to it. He grabbed up my prick and poured his lips over my hood, engulfed my shaft with his mouth. I shuddered with joy, the wet, wicked, heated sensation making my head spin.

He swallowed my beef stick almost right down to the balls, then bobbed up, back down again, sucking on my prick. I groaned, gripping his rod at the base, pushing my fist up into his sack. Then I pulled him down into my mouth, taking his cap inside, half his shaft. He shuddered, his cock jumping in my mouth.

199

He tasted just as delicious as it looked. His dick filled my mouth with satisfaction, hood bulging the back of my throat. I moved my head like he was, sucking on his meat, lips pulling, tongue dragging. We were eating each other's cocks, ravenous men consummating their lust. There weren't too many cooks in this steaming kitchen, two just enough, the recipe just right.

DeShawn moaned when I scraped his shaft with my teeth. His voice vibrated up my dong and all through my body. I was ablaze with the sucking sensations, ready to blow hot sauce down the man's throat.

But he beat me to it again. He spasmed, his cock surging in my mouth, then erupting. Hot sperm blasted the back of my throat, thick and salty. I gulped for all I was worth. Then spasmed myself, orgasm detonating in my body and brain, exploding out of the tip of my sucked-upon dick.

I flooded DeShawn's mouth, making him swallow hot gooey goodness like I was swallowing, my sucking lips sealed tight to his shaft, milking the man. We came over and over, with a mind and ball-blowing intensity and quantity that satiated even our starving souls.

Lugo the asshole ended up canning me over the order he'd screwed up. I never saw DeShawn again, quickly getting a better job in another part of town. But that spicy scent of pizza baking, the warming heat from the ovens, gives me a hard-on every time, everything on it.

PLAY IT AS HE LIES
By Landon Dixon

I had the pics spread out on my desk – a girl caught red-snatched in the middle of a gang-bang – and was giving them the eyeball as I gave my cock a hand. My dick was thrusting up tall out of the opening in my pants, clutched in my shifting mitt, getting a rubdown of the jacking variety. And my eyes weren't on the pretty nude girl at the center of the five-man pound party; I was ogling the five men in action in the full color candid pics.

Three were black, one Hispanic, one Asian. All uniformly built. They were starkly naked as the girl, muscles clenched, cocks jutting, fucking, fondling, getting sucked by the creamy center of the orgy. I stroked my unholstered rod just as torrid, enjoying the spectacle for a second time, just as hot upon reflection.

See, I'd snapped the incriminating photos, on behalf of an elderly client who suspected his young trophy wife was back doing the hot sheet samba with her dance instructor ex-boyfriend. The good news for the horny old geezer was that the ex wasn't anywhere in the picture. The bad news was that almost every other more-than-able-bodied male in the Lower Mainland was.

The tramp'd had a busy week. I had more pictorial evidence of how she passed her time: getting her ass fucked by the family chauffeur; a dp threesome with a pair of lawn care specialists who also did carpet; a lesbian daisy-chain that linked half of the neighborhood wives together where it cunted most. The rip-roaring gang-bang was just the capper on the week, all those studly gents capturing my one-eyed attention all over again. My hand flew up and down my pipe, polishing rigid.

"There's a woman here to see you," Danton bleated, barging into my office.

He hardly batted a long, curled eyelash at the sight of me pushed back in my chair with my legs spread, cock at full mast, hand pumping the prime, X-rated pictures scattered all over my work desk. The guy understood me, and my needs. He'd been with me two years, his long, lithe form, Old Wave haircut, twinkling brown eyes and lush chocolate lips, earning him a secretarial spot in my investigations business.

He demonstrated his skills now, loping around the desk in his tight, pinstriped pants and folding down to his knees, spinning my swivel chair his way so that my cock jutted out right before him. He took dicktation, brushing my hand aside and clamping his own light, hot touch onto my dong. His long, slim fingers laced around the base of my boiled shaft. "Got another caseload, huh?" he quipped, voice as tinkly as his strut. He tickled the tip of my dick with the tip of his tongue.

I jerked, touched deep inside.

He'd left the door open. But the angle was such that I couldn't see the dame cooling her heels in the closet-sized outer office, and she couldn't see Danton heating my prong. So I sifted my fingers into the guy's soft, kinky hair, applied downward pressure on his noggin. His lips flowered over my hood, poured down my shaft.

"Yeah, baby!" I growled, thrusting upwards, filling the man's mouth as he inhaled in the opposite direction.

Danton didn't only work hard, he worked deep. His lips kissed up against my belly and balls, dark nose burrowing into my ginger pubes, my cock bulging his cheeks and bloating his throat, beating away.

He spun his misty glims upwards, locked them onto my widened grey orbs. He batted his lashes demurely, face stuffed full of cock, hot air blowing out of his delicate nostrils and flooding my groin. Me and my dick were enveloped in luscious heat and wetness, an oral steam bath. I curled my fingers up tight in Danton's hair, already over-stimulated from the recent case review, this intimate chin-wag sucking me over the edge.

"Christ! I'm coming!" I grunted, giving the snake-charmer fair warning.

His eyes lit up with delight, throat and mouth clamping even tighter, lips sealing shaft. Giving me the green light.

I quivered, the pressure on my locked-down dick and boiling balls incredible, his mouth a melting pot. Danton moved his head just a little, sucked a centimeter. And I bucked and blasted, blew salty, sweet exultation down the guy's throat.

He didn't even have to swallow, the jets of joy from my bent, buried cock shooting right down into his stomach, to join the sperm cocktail he'd probably already had for breakfast back at his place. I bounced around in my chair like it was a hot seat, gushing my praise for a deep-throat well done.

He jerked his head up and shook off my hands, sucked up a final long string of saliva and cum and licked his lips, then leapt to his feet. "Her name's Mrs. Singh, says her husband has been kidnapped."

I shook the orgasmic haze out of my head, nodded curtly. I toweled my dick off with a tissue and tucked and zipped. "Send her in."

Then I added, "And, Danton, give yourself the rest of the afternoon off. You might be coming down with a sore throat."

He formed those blowjob lips of his into a smile, used them to say, "I wouldn't think of it. Who knows? Another case development might spring up that I can help you with again."

Like I said, a good, hard worker, especially when I'm good and hard.

Mrs. Singh sat down in one of the chairs across from my desk, a short, dusky-skinned woman with large brown eyes and a plain Jane face, fleshy padding all over her body.

"My husband, Sanjay," she stated, "has been kidnapped. Here is the text message that I received from his cellphone yesterday morning."

She handed me a sheet of paper. It read: "$200,000 or your husband dies. Instructions to follow. No cops."

"Yesterday?" I posited, raising a copper eyebrow.

She didn't flinch. "I had to consult with my family first. They are very wealthy, you see, while Sanjay is nothing but a humble provincial civil servant."

I got the picture. Louder and clearer when the woman showed me a snapshot of her beloved. Sanjay had a thin, coffee-colored face, a cheesy black mustache and wavy black hair, thin nose and lips, weak chin and sad eyes. I never forget a face. I'd seen that mug once before, not too long ago, at a place called Mr. Velvet Pants, a raunchy gay bar on the tattered fringe of the Downtown Eastside.

"My family has reluctantly agreed to pay the ransom," Mrs. Singh said. "You will deliver it. Unless ... you can do something to prevent the transaction – for which my family would be most grateful."

I nodded, crossing my hands in my lap, over my re-energized cock. The memory of my one visit to Mr. Velvet Pants, the obtuse mention of reward, had aroused my attention once again. "You're happily married, Mrs. Singh?"

"Of course."

I puckered a smile. "I'll get right on your case."

# # # # #

Mr. Velvet Pants was pulling pretty rough trade for a rainy late-afternoon. Three guys in leathers, two bears busting out of their plaid shirts and blue work overalls, and a city councilor. The place was little more than a room with no view, bar occupying one side of the square, blue velvet chairs and velvet-topped tables and innuendo a blind man could read scattered about the rest of the room.

I flashed Sanjay's picture at the bearded barman, along with a double-sawbuck chaser. The politician made a beeline for the backdoor at that point, figuring me for a real cop. The barman shrugged his beefy shoulders and gave his beard a shake. The leathermen crowded in.

"Who're you looking for, sweetheart?" one of them asked. A guy decked out like Marlon Brando from *The Wild One*, complete with little white cap balanced on the back of his head. "We know most of the regulars."

I showed him the pic, the dough. He nodded, pointed to one of the doors marked 'Men.' We adjourned our discussion to more commodious surroundings.

The three lugs crowded in on me even closer in the cramped, semen-stained and scented surroundings, hanging the nasty on their leathery features now. "What the fuck you after, anyway, asshole!?" the Wild One snarled, punching a pointed digit into my chest. "Sanjay's a good guy. We don't like …"

I kneed him in the unprotected groin, banged my right fist off the tip of his anguished, bent-over physiognomy. He snapped upright, then fainted downward. The other two guys rushed me. I chopped one across the throat, making him bob for his Adam's apple, gasping. The other drew a left hook to the right kidney, a chop across the side of his neck. He crumpled down onto the faded yellow floor tiles.

"You wanna play rough, it'll save me some bucks," I grated, pinning the one still-standing leatherman up against a toilet stall wall with a forearm across his bruised throat.

His eyes watered, blinking with pain, as I shot my other hand down to his chaps, twisted his balls this way and that. "He rents a motel room – by the month!" leatherman squeaked. "The Snowball, on Burrard."

I yanked his nuts down to the tearing off point, slamming my body weight behind the armbar.

"Room 21!" he squealed. "A place to get away from the wife!"

I let him breathe ragged, rancid air again, told him to grow a bigger pair or ditch the leathers.

Advice free-of-charge.

# # # # #

The Snowball Motel was seedier than the Stanley Park Aviary. A two-story, rectangular hunk of lime-green stucco and purple metal nestled within twenty miles of the foot of Grouse Mountain. The freeway traffic was just as loud as the color scheme.

I rented Room 23, one over on the right, put a speckled water glass up to the wall, then an ear. I heard various voices on the other side of the plywood, couldn't quite make out what they were saying.

I stood up on the lumpy bed and carefully drilled a hole through the wall with a silenced pocket drill, fed a length of thin cable through the hole. The cable had a camera mounted on the tip. The picture came through on my laptop in roiling Technicolor: Sanjay getting fucked ass and mouth by his "captors."

I sat down on the bed, set the laptop up on my knees, drew my rod out of my pants. All three men were totally nude, Sanjay positioned on all-fours on the floor, huge cock in his mouth, churning back and forth, huge cock in his ass, banging in and out. The guy's brown skin was burnished with sweat, ass cheeks rippling with wicked impact, face cheeks billowing with awesome reaction.

The man reaming his butt was big and broad and black-haired, skin smooth and black as onyx, body chiseled just as hard. His thick fingers dug into Sanjay's narrow waist, his thick cock sawing manhole full-bore.

The man on the other sucking end was just as broad and built and dark, but with a blossomed orange turban, a trimmed mustache and nutduster. His cock was long and lean and veined, gleaming with spit, not lube. He gripped Sanjay's head and oiled that dong in and out of the gasping guy's drooling mouth.

I cranked my cock, getting the picture. Poor Sanjay, literally, was forced to exist on a civil servant's salary, while his wife's family had oodles of caboodle. He was gay; his wife didn't know it. So, he'd faked a kidnapping to get his hands on some of that in-law dough, man-meat for the rest of his natural sex life. He'd blow town with his booty and two male lovers once they and he were paid off.

A nice trick, if you can pull it off. But he hadn't counted on this dick, and my dick.

The rump-rider growled, howled, tossing his head back and torquing Sanjay's ass, blasting chute full of man-juice, burst after brain-shattering, ball-emptying burst. Just as the face-filler let loose with his own cry of ecstasy, spurted mouthfuls of semen in soul-jarring spasms.

Sanjay took it ass and mouth, like a true co-conspirator.

I busted through the door before the two beef boys could repackage their tools, a real, metal rod in my mitt now. "Coming-out party's over, lovers," I gritted at them. "Weigh dick and hit the bricks. I see you again and you're both going to jail – extortion."

They looked dazed, decided to take my offer to take air, the .38 the clincher. I kept them covered as they clothed, crowded outside. Then I slammed the door and locked it, swiveled my sights onto the still-naked, doggy-positioned Sanjay.

"Okay, sweet cheeks, here's how it's going to go down. Your boyfriends are out. But the fake kidnapping gag stays. Only, now I'm getting half of the geetus."

His eyes gaped like his mouth and asshole. "Fake!? They really did kidnap me! They-they heard me complaining about all of the money my wife's family has – at Mr. Velvet Pants – and they were trying to get a piece of it, like I never can." He hung his head, his cock.

I chewed on what he'd babbled. It tasted legit, had the ring of authenticity. Still … "And a piece of you?"

He looked up, sheepish as a shepherd. "Well, the Stockholm Syndrome set in fairly quickly, I guess. They were such polite, good-looking young men, you see."

"Yeah, I saw."

I sighed and holstered my gun, pulled out my other shooter. I wasn't about to get mixed up in a real, legitimate kidnapping. Even by Canadian coddling legal standards, that could draw some serious jail time.

So, I took some consolation by getting Sanjay to wrap his chocolate lips around my swollen pole, suck fast and furious. He owed me something for rescuing his ass.

He eagerly gripped my thighs, dove his head back and forth. His throat capacity was enormous, man-sized, like Danton's. My dick bent down his maw, the guy wet-vaccing tight and righteous. I grasped his thick raven hair and pumped my hips, helping him suck. He had my balls popping like a Saturday night bingo machine in mere minutes.

"Onto the bed!" I rasped. "Assume the position."

He climbed up onto the mattress, presented his ripe, round bottom to me. I got on my knees at his rear, greased my spit-slickened dong with some of the lube the kidnappers had thoughtfully left behind, some of the semen still in his ass. Then I poked his dark hole with my puffy cap, popped through and inside. I sunk every inch of stiffened shaft into Sanjay's superheated chute, and he and I and the bed all groaned.

He gripped my dick with his butt muscles. I grasped his waist and stoked up to ramming speed, pistoning deep and true, setting his pudding buttocks to gyrating with my banging thighs. He clutched the ratty bedspread, chewed on it, hanging a hand on his own flapping hard-on and jacking.

I pumped like a madman. My face and body burned, my plugging cock surging come-hard in Sanjay's sucking anus. He shuddered, whimpered, jumped, fisting out more semen onto the already sperm-streaked bedspread. As I savagely drove his ass to blast-off.

I jerked, jolted by blistering orgasm, cock exploding in the man's shivering butt. I yelled out loud enough to bring the Law and the wafer-thin walls down, dousing Sanjay's bowels with spray after spray of white-hot cum. Case cracked, crack encased.

# # # # #

Mrs. Singh and her family proved just as cheap as Sanjay had told me. I presented her with one husband safe and sound, her family with a savings of $200,000, and she presented me with a cheque for $325 – one day's work plus motel room rental.

It was up to Sanjay to pay the piper. I blackmailed the guy for a modest 10 Gs – cough up the dough via payroll deduction or I'd blow the whistle with the missus about his gay-play proclivities. I had the hard drive, firsthand testimony and financial need to back it up.

Danton's one of the most expensive secretaries in the business, after all. And I don't "come" cheap, either.

THE EDITOR

MARCUS ANTHONY is a writer and editor, residing in Newport News, Virginia. He *is* the color sexy.

earing any underwear. "Excuse me," I said, having a hard time lo

linded by that bulge in his crotch, "but don't I know you?" "May

ind of t   bou

with Ray   God

t loser?   in?"

aid. "Lik   s stro

ce body   e on

lly, he l   I ev

a up to t   any i

istaking   ie sa

n, I coul   ery l

ood rac   me s

ing with   e in

we go   beh

vill see u   in p

ed?" he   vent

privacy.   grab

-hard. I

k, tracii   t, so

ed it, ha

with m   bing

bbing, I   n co

he sound of unzipping filled the small space. I don't know who's

, but before I knew it, I had his rod in my hand, and mine was in l

nt to do?" he asked, his tone challenging. I knew exactly, and san

CPSIA information can be obtained at www.ICGtesting.com
Printed in the USA
LVOW121657020413

327240LV00007B/855/P